"Sooner or later, the lightning comes to us all."

—Gregory Maguire,
A Lion Among Men

BRIAN S

WOND

A Novel in Wo

SCHOLASTIC P

LZNICK

ER
TRUCK

s and Pictures

SS · NEW YORK

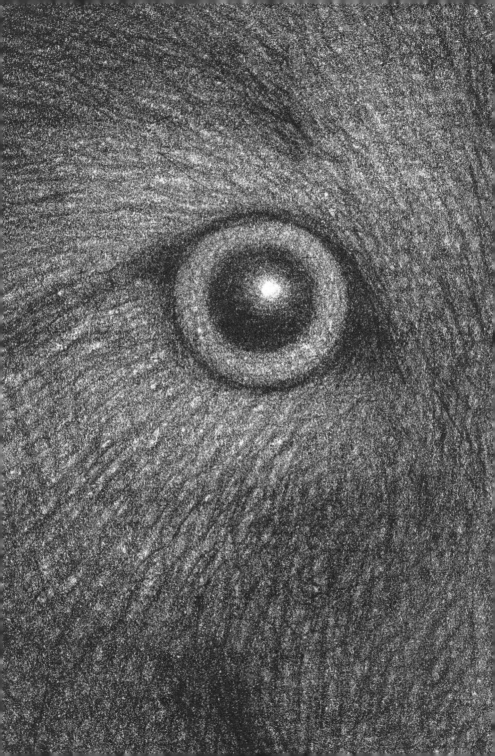

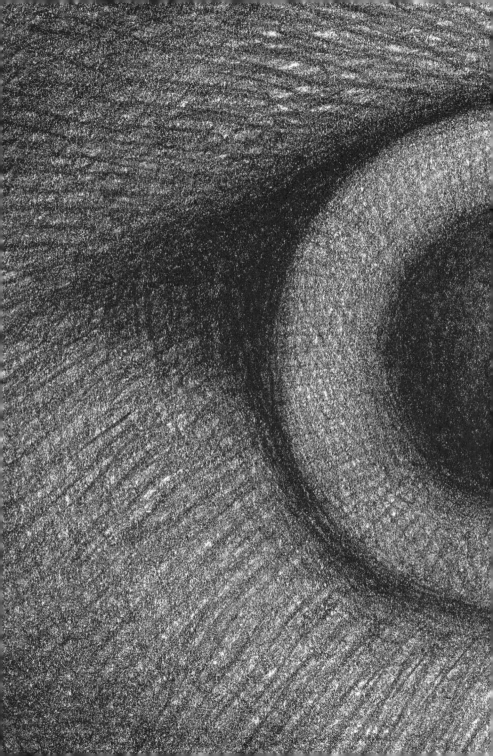

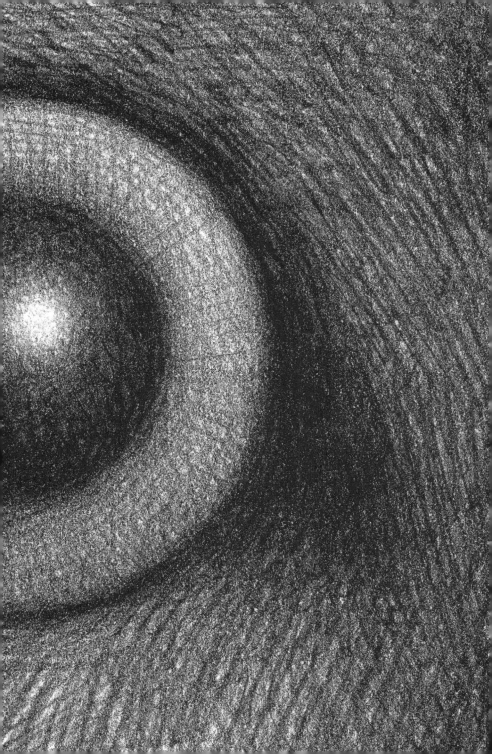

GUNFLINT LAI

JUNE

, MINNESOTA

977

PART ONE

Something hit Ben Wilson and he opened his eyes. The wolves had been chasing him again and his heart was pounding. He sat up in the dark room and rubbed his arm. He picked up the shoe his cousin had thrown at him and dropped it on the floor.

"That hurt, Robby!"

Robby muttered a few words.

"What?" Ben asked.

"What? What? Can't you hear me? Are you deaf?"

Robby, along with practically everyone else on Gunflint Lake, knew that Ben had been born deaf in one ear, but he still thought it was funny to ask Ben this all the time, even in the middle of the night. He repeated himself for Ben. "I said, stop yelling in your sleep!"

In the corner of the room, Robby's hunting rifle glinted in the moonlight. Piled nearby were his fishing rod, pocketknife, bow, arrows, handmade spears, and slingshots of varying sizes. Robby seemed to go out of his way to collect dangerous things.

Ben lay back down on the old cot squeezed between the dresser and the window. The electric fan was broken, and both boys were shirtless and sweating in the summer heat. Their blankets were thrown uselessly to the side. Their hair was matted to their foreheads.

Ben's hands were still shaking from the dream. Ever since the accident, the wolves had appeared, galloping across the moonlit snow, red tongues wagging and white teeth glistening. He couldn't figure out why they were stalking him, because he used to love wolves. He and his mom had even seen one once from the front porch of their house. The wolf had looked beautiful and mysterious, like it had stepped out of a storybook.

Outside, the wind picked up and rustled through the leaves on the giant trees surrounding the house. Voices droned from Robby's CB radio, which he insisted stay on all night. It didn't bother Ben that much. Being deaf in one ear had its advantages: He could sleep with his good ear on the pillow to block out all the noise. Ben used a similar trick in school. He'd lean his good ear on his hand when he wanted to tune out his teacher or his classmates. It made it easier to read the books about outer space that he hid in his desk.

"I wish I didn't have to share my room with you anymore," Robby said before drifting back to sleep.

Ben silently agreed.

A familiar noise caught his attention and he put his good ear against the wall.

"It's been three months since she died, Jenny. We've got to talk about selling it."

Ben knew right away his aunt Jenny and uncle Steve were talking about his house again.

"Elaine loved that house, Steve," Aunt Jenny countered. "And our grandfather *built* these houses and the little guest cabin. It's not so easy to sell something that's part of our family. Can't we just leave it be for now?"

Ben could picture his aunt tightening her ponytail as she said this, a habit she shared with Robby's older sister, Janet. His mom had done it as well, when she had something serious to say.

"We're going to have to sell it sooner or later," Uncle Steve said. "It can't sit there untouched forever. We have bills to pay, and now we have Ben."

"You've booked hunting and fishing trips with three lodges for nearly the entire season, and I'm cooking at Gunflint Lodge. We'll be fine."

"Yes, but the money doesn't last all year."

"Summer's just starting, Steve. Do we really have to worry about this now?"

A long silence followed.

Growing up, Ben had never thought about who owned his house. It had always belonged to him and his mom. But now it seemed as if it was his aunt and uncle's. Why wasn't it still Ben's? Could a kid even own a house?

After the funeral in March, Ben had figured he'd be able to go back into his house whenever he wanted, considering it was only eighty-three steps away from his cousins'. But the more time passed, the more afraid he was to walk through the front door again without his mom there to greet him on the other side.

There weren't many houses on the lake. His house and his cousins' house were the two closest to one another. Ben missed the cluttered coziness of his house—the little tables, mismatched chairs, old clocks, quotes his mom had carefully clipped and taped to the refrigerator, prints of her favorite artwork, rusted cogs and wheels and other interesting things Ben had scavenged on their walks around the lake and in town, their record collection, the stone fireplace, their prized moose antler found along the Gunflint Trail, and of course all of their books, which spilled out of the bookcases and were stacked in piles around the house.

If his aunt and uncle sold his house, wondered Ben, what would happen to all his stuff? What would happen to his mom's stuff? Who would live there? Maybe he could move all their things to the little guest cabin. When the cousins were little they used to play there if a visitor wasn't using it. They pretended it was a witch's castle or a pirate ship. Even though it was only a hundred yards farther down the lake, it felt miles away from the grown-ups. That all seemed like another lifetime now.

The argument between his aunt and uncle had subsided and the clock down the hall chimed midnight. Unable to keep his eyes closed, Ben reached beneath his cot for his red plastic flashlight and the wood box he kept hidden there.

The box was about the size of his math textbook. It was shiny brown and smooth to the touch. The bottom was covered in soft green felt. On the lid was an engraving of a wolf. One of the artists in town had made it, and Ben's mom had given it to him for Christmas last year. The box, the flashlight, and two suitcases full of his clothes were the only things he'd brought with him when he moved into Robby's room.

Ben turned on the flashlight, pulled a key from the pocket of his pants, which lay folded on the floor, and opened the small brass lock on the front of the box. One at a time, he touched the little items inside.

He had organized them between cardboard dividers, giving each one a special section. Among other things, he had several oddly shaped twigs, his last baby tooth, a little plastic game piece he'd found behind the school with his friend Billy—who always teased him for picking up garbage—a bird skull, and a fossil called a stromatolite that he'd discovered while hiking the ridges near Gunflint Lake. In the bottom right-hand corner of the cardboard grid were two small, bumpy gray stones. Ben picked up one and turned it in his palm. When he had showed them to his mom, she told him that these stones, called ejecta, as well as the entire area where they lived, had been created nearly two billion years ago, by a meteorite crash across the lake in Canada.

After that, Ben became fascinated by the stars and outer space, so his mom brought him to the library where she worked and showed him all the books about the night sky. Sitting beside her at her big orange desk, its papers and books piled taller than he'd been at the time, he'd found a diagram of the Big Dipper, which pointed to the North Star. The North Star was the last star in the tail of the Little Dipper, and the book said that travelers had used this star for centuries to find their way when they were lost. "If you are ever lost," his mom had said when he showed her the book, "just find the North Star and it will lead you home."

His mom smiled, and pointed to a bulletin board next

to her desk. Unlike the refrigerator at home, it had just one quote taped to it.

Ben read it out loud: "'We are all in the gutter, but some of us are looking at the stars.'"

Because his mom was the town librarian, Ben was used to being surrounded by quotes from books, many of which he didn't fully understand. But this one struck him as particularly strange.

He thought about it for a moment, came up with nothing, then said, "What does *that* mean?"

His mom smiled and shrugged.

He was sure she knew *exactly* what it meant, but she liked him to figure out things for himself.

"Was it written by an astronomer?" he asked.

She shrugged again, but Ben could tell the answer was there, just out of reach behind her eyes.

Over the next week, Ben read all the books about stars his mom had found for him, and then convinced her to let him paint his room black. At the general store in town, he bought an armful of glow-in-the-dark stars and covered the walls and ceiling of his room with them. He put the Big Dipper, the Little Dipper, and the North Star directly over his bed. His mom surprised him with an old telescope she bought with money from her rainy-day fund. He placed it right next to his window and gazed through it every night before bed. Once, when Billy came over, he looked at all the space stuff and said, "Oh, I get it . . . you're an alien." Ben had laughed along with Billy, but every time he looked through his telescope after that, he had the same thought: I'm an alien.

Ben put the bumpy gray stone back in its little compartment. For a moment, he wondered again about the quote, and what his mom thought it meant, but it passed out of his mind as he lifted a bird skull from the box. He'd found the skull on one of his weekend walks with his mom on the Gunflint Trail. He ran his fingers over the smooth dome of the head and the sharp point of the beak. His mom had made him research what kind of bird it was, and he found out it was a waxwing. He read all the bird books in his mom's library and could now identify twenty-three different species just by looking at their bones. In a book about the birds of Minnesota, he'd come across a reference to the Duluth Museum and their collection of bird skeletons. "Can we go there, Mom?" he'd asked. "It's only four hours away." His mom had tightened her ponytail and said she'd think about it. The more Ben read about the museum's collections, the more he wanted to go to Duluth. He begged her for months, until one day she said, "Is that what you want for your birthday this summer? A trip to Duluth?"

"Yes!" Ben practically jumped into the air.

"Don't get too excited about it. We'll see. . . ."

Ben wiped his hand across his eyes, as if he were rubbing away the vision of Duluth. He put the bird skull back into the box and thought of all the time he'd spent at his mom's library after school, reading up on birds or outer space and doing homework. If only he'd been there the day of the accident instead of sick at home. Surely he could have done something to help her. At the very least he would have seen the snow and ice accumulating on the road and reminded her to put on her seat belt. How he wished he could go back in time.

Ben took a deep breath and closed his eyes, knowing he'd never get to Duluth. His aunt and uncle couldn't afford a trip, especially now that they had to take care of him. Even though he loved them, he didn't feel at home with his aunt and uncle. But where else could he live? He didn't have any other family. His grandparents had died when he was very little, and he'd never known anything about his dad. The one time he had hinted around the subject to his mom, she'd tightened her ponytail a few times and then undid it altogether. As her long black hair spilled down around her shoulders, her eyes filled with tears. Ben had never seen his mother cry before, and it startled him, so he didn't ask again. Right afterward she'd put on her favorite record and played a mysterious song called "Space Oddity," about an astronaut named Major Tom who gets lost in space. She used to listen to the song over and over again. With her eyes closed, she'd place the palm of her hand against the fabric of the speaker, so she could feel it vibrate against her skin.

In bed that night, staring up into the glowing stars glued to his ceiling, Ben had imagined that Major Tom was his father, and he found himself wondering: What did he look like? Did he know about Ben? Would he ever come back to Earth?

Ben opened his eyes and stared into the small circle of light from the flashlight that illuminated the box on his lap. Ever since his mom died, Major Tom had been on his mind. He liked to pretend that Major Tom arrived in a spaceship behind his cousins' house. While his whole family watched, Ben would climb aboard and disappear into the night sky. He knew it was a childish daydream, but it wouldn't go away.

From the box, he picked up a little turtle made of glued-together seashells. It felt smooth and cool in his hand. His mom had given it to him when he started third grade. It had been sort of a joke between them. When he was little, she used to call him Turtle because he was so quiet. "You know, Turtle," she'd said before they left for school, "you shouldn't be such a turtle. . . . Remember to stick your neck out. . . . Speak up, be brave."

His mom ran her fingers down his cheek until they touched the underside of his chin, and she lifted his face so their eyes met. "Don't be afraid to look people in the eye when they talk to you, okay?"

"Okay," he said, holding her gaze.

"That's better."

Ben held the turtle tightly in his palm and laid the box and flashlight on his cot. He opened the bug screen in the window and leaned out. The air felt thick against his skin. He looked at his home, sitting empty, through the trees. A mosquito buzzed near his good ear. With his head turned slightly to the right, he could just make out a trucker on Robby's radio talking about an approaching storm. Ben looked up at the sky. It was growing overcast, but a few stars still twinkled through the gaps between the clouds.

He had believed his mother when she told him he'd never be lost as long as he could find the North Star. But now that she was gone, he realized it wasn't true.

The mysterious quote from his mom's bulletin board echoed again in his mind.

We are all in the gutter, but some of us are looking at the stars.

HOBOKEN

OCTO

NEW JERSEY

R 1927

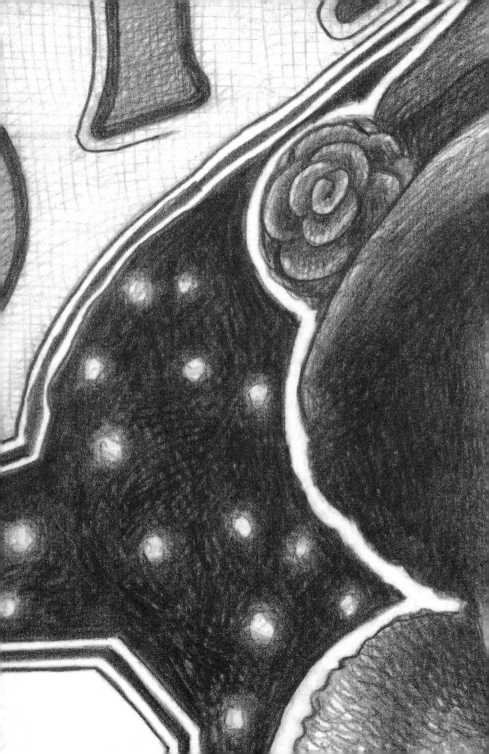

February 1927
Happy Birthday Rose
love Walter
Miss Rose Kincaid
168 River Street
Hoboken, N.J.
OCTOBER
MOVIESTAR MAGAZINE
19
CHILDREN CRY FOR
Mama
CASTO
Mother!

Happy Birthday Rose
love Walter
168 River Street
Hoboken, N.J.
OCTOBER
MOVIESTAR MAGAZINE
19
CHILDREN CRY FOR
Mama
CASTO
CASTORIA
Mother!

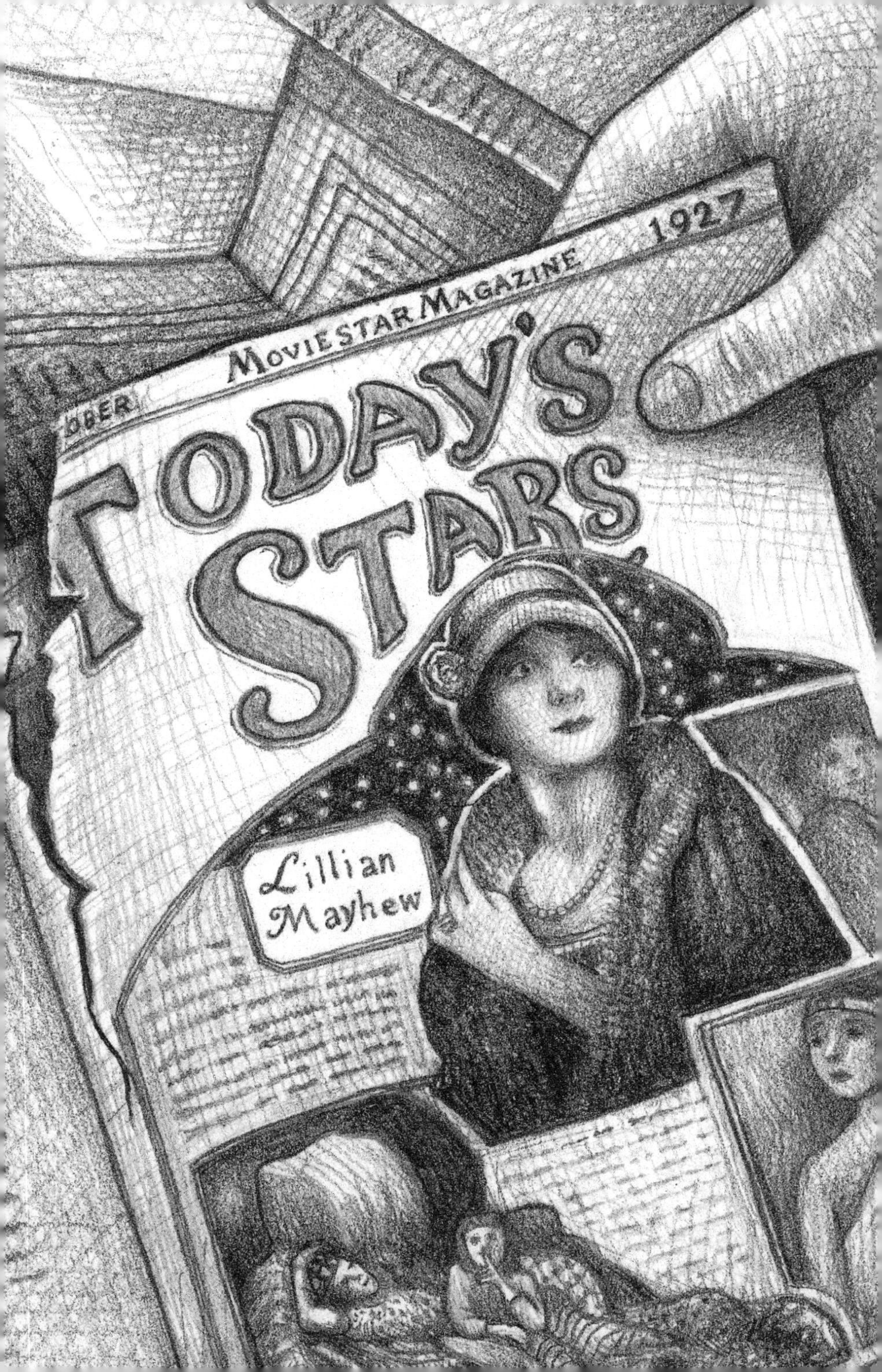
1927
MOVIESTAR MAGAZINE
TODAY'S STARS
Lillian Mayhew

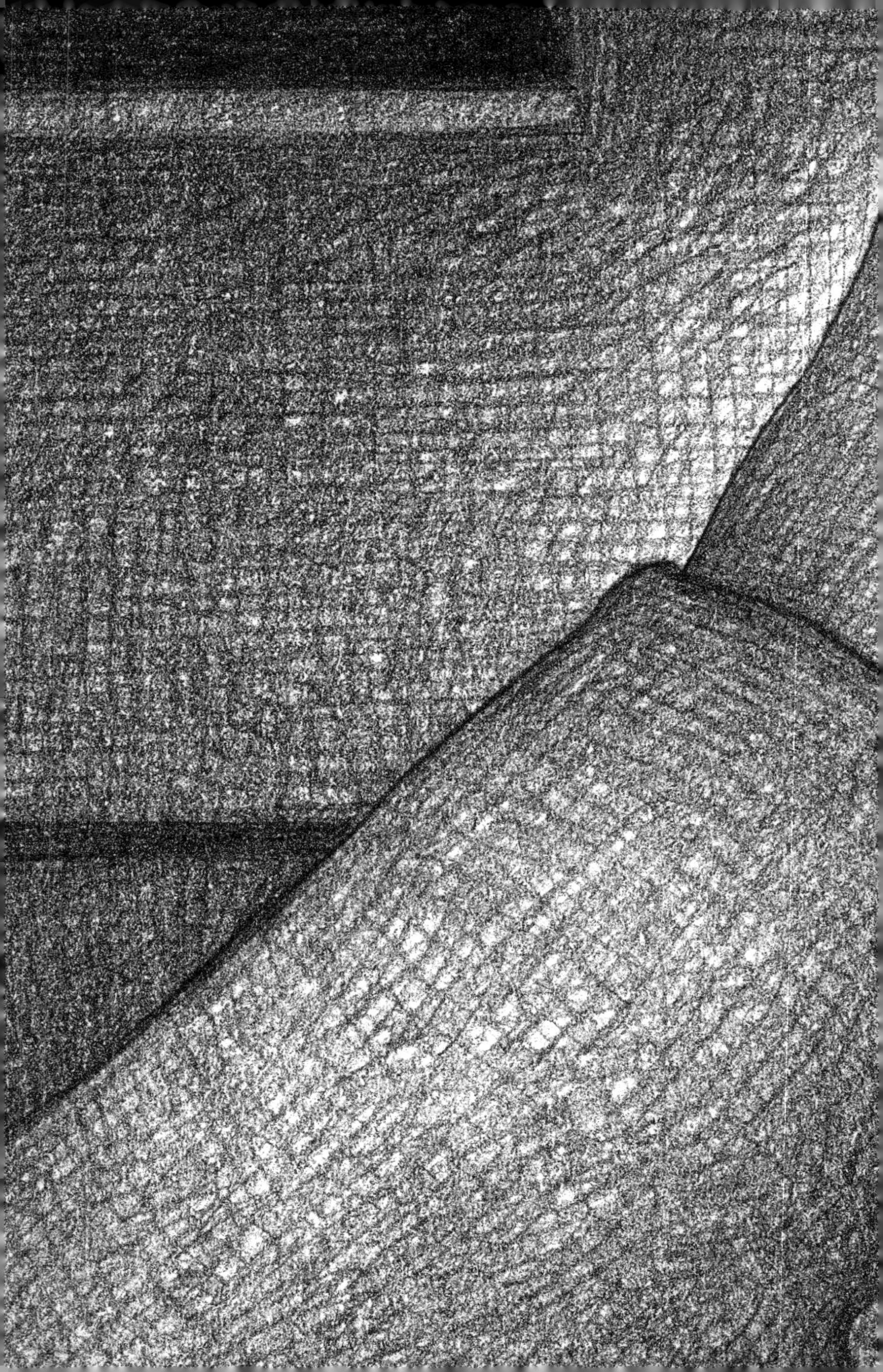

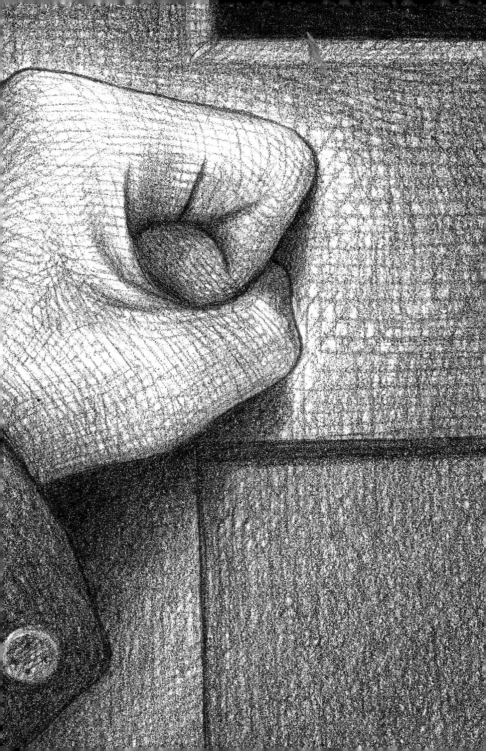

Ben leaned against Robby's windowsill until it made a red line across his chest. He watched the clouds roll in. He thought about the times when the aurora borealis, the northern lights, appeared in the night sky. Everyone along the lake would call one another, no matter what time it was, so they could watch the strange shimmering curtains vibrating above them. Even though his mom had quit smoking two summers ago, Ben vividly remembered the smell of her cigarettes as they stood outside. She'd cross her arms and blow the smoke out the side of her mouth. When the air was cold enough, Ben would cross his arms and blow his foggy breath out the side of his mouth as well, which always made her laugh. Then she would open her jacket so Ben could stand inside it with her, and for hours they would stare heavenward at the beautiful colors in the sky.

A sudden streak of light interrupted Ben's memory. Wide-eyed, he watched from the ledge of Robby's window as a shooting star blazed between the clouds and disappeared. He made a wish about his mom, one that he knew could never come true.

Ben hadn't realized how tightly he'd been gripping the seashell turtle until he felt it digging into his skin. He almost cried out, but he caught himself, not wanting to wake up Robby again.

That's when Ben noticed something very strange. In the black silhouette of his house, eighty-three steps away, a light had come on. The curtains in his mom's room glowed a bright yellow.

Ben stared in disbelief.

Feeling dizzy, he placed the turtle in the box, locked it, and tucked it back under the cot. His heart was pounding as he put on an old tank top and slid into his sneakers without bothering to lace them up.

He grabbed the red flashlight and slipped silently out of his cousins' house.

Water lapped at the dock, and the boats clacked against one another. A loon called across the night, and the stones of Gunflint Lake glittered faintly in the darkness. The woods at night were always spooky, and the weak beam of the flashlight didn't stretch very far. Ben kept moving toward his house, where the one glowing window beckoned, staring back through the darkness like an unblinking eye. Under a vault of shaking black branches, he ran.

The doors to his house, like nearly all the doors along the lake, were unlocked. Ben quietly entered through the back, into the kitchen. He moved his small beam of light around the room. The flowers and food from the funeral had been cleared out, but the owl-shaped cookie jar sat on the counter with its head off, the way it always had. The junk drawer remained closed crookedly. The refrigerator was still covered with his mom's favorite quotes. It was like entering a museum of his old life.

Ben realized that he could hear music playing softly in the distance. He turned his head to hear it more clearly and a chill went down his spine.

"This is Major Tom to ground control;
I'm stepping thro' the door,
And I'm floating in a most peculiar way.

And the stars look very different today
For here am I sitting in a tin can far above the
world. . . ."

Ben heard footsteps. He turned his good ear toward the direction he thought the sound was coming from . . . somewhere near his mother's room, he guessed.

Ben had never really believed in ghosts, although some of the stories his mom had read to him when he was younger had kept him up at night. He tiptoed slowly down the hall to his mom's room, the blood pounding in his head. A faint smell of cigarette smoke grew stronger as he got closer.

Ben paused in the hallway, dizzy with fear. *"You shouldn't be such a turtle."*

He inched closer until he was right outside her door. He turned off the flashlight and put it in his back pocket.

The door was open a crack, and he could see the framed Van Gogh print—a big black tree and a swirling night sky with golden stars. A shadow moved across the room.

Ben thought about the shooting star and the impossible wish he'd made. With a trembling hand, he slowly pushed open the door.

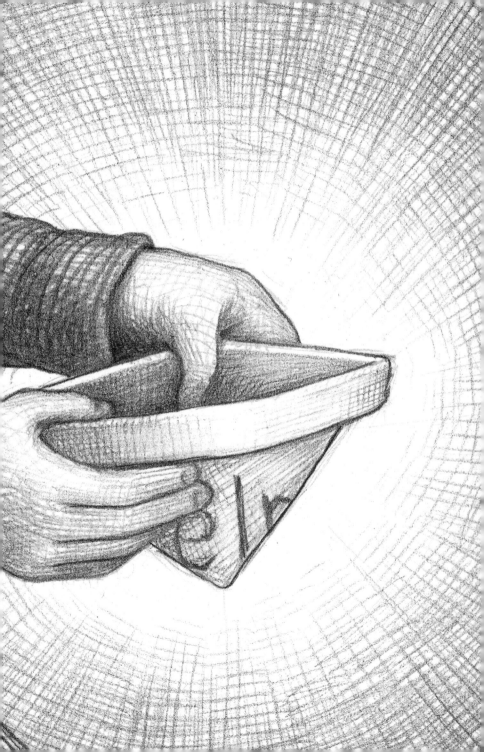

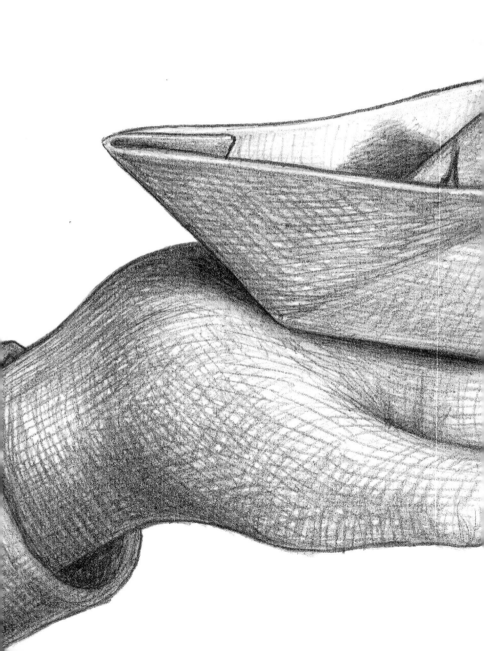

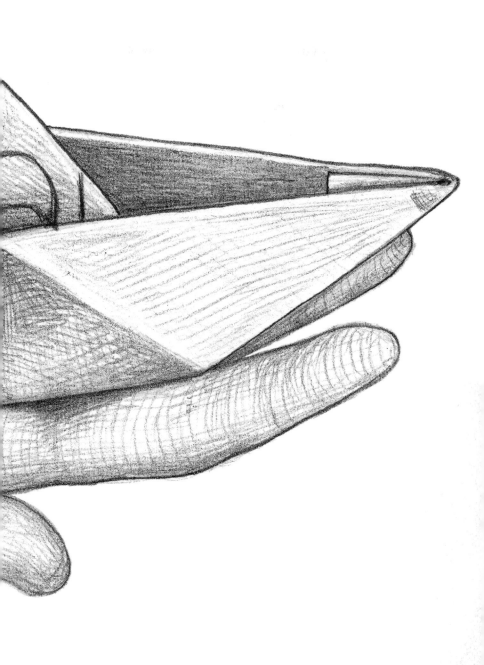

She was standing with her back to him, wearing her favorite skirt, dancing slowly to the music. A cigarette dangled carelessly in her left hand. Ben felt his knees buckle, and when he tried to steady himself, the door suddenly opened wider, making a loud creaking sound.

His mother whipped around.

Ben gasped.

It wasn't his mother at all.

It was his cousin Janet. She was wearing his mother's clothes and smoking her old brand of cigarettes.

"What are you doing here?" Janet cried, her eyes wide with shock and embarrassment.

"What are *you* doing here?" answered Ben. "This isn't your house! Those aren't your things!" He felt stupid for thinking, even for a second, that this could have been his mother. He wiped his eyes quickly so Janet wouldn't see the tears.

The color drained from Janet's face. "I knew I shouldn't have turned on the lamp. Benji, I—"

"You *smoke*?"

Janet looked at the cigarette in her hand as if she had only then realized it was there. She stubbed it out quickly in the glass she was using for an ashtray. "No! Well . . . yes," she said. "I mean . . . only sometimes. It's just . . . oh god, please don't tell my parents. They'll kill me!"

"Why are you here? I don't understand. You're wearing my mom's *clothes*."

"Oh, Benji, I'm sorry. This was supposed to be my secret! I—" Janet sat on the bed, buried her face in her hands, and started to cry.

Ben didn't know what else to say. He found himself feeling sorry for her. Janet had always made an effort to be nice to him. She was the one who had found him hiding in his mom's closet after the funeral. Instead of telling anyone, or making fun of him the way Robby would have, she climbed inside and sat beside him. The two of them had cried together and held on to each other without saying a word.

Janet looked up at him from the bed. She tightened her ponytail and took a breath. "Benji, I know this is your mom's room. It's just . . ." She paused and reached around to the back of her neck, unclasped a silver locket, and placed it in the jewelry box. Ben had never seen the necklace before, but then again, his mom had never worn much jewelry.

A tin coffee can sat on the bed. Janet opened it and handed it to Ben.

"I found this. I thought you might want it."

The coffee can was filled with cash. It had to be his mom's rainy-day fund. Ben handed it back to Janet.

"That's probably a lot of money, Ben. You should keep it."

He shook his head and pushed the can back toward Janet, who set it down on the bed. She picked up her own clothes. "I'll . . . I'll go change in the bathroom," she said nervously.

After she left, Ben looked around the room in a daze. It was just the way he remembered it: the desk with his mom's papers, her bed, which still had her indentation in it, and the piles of library books on her nightstand. He should probably return those, he thought. His mom would have been unhappy knowing she had overdue books.

"Benji?"

Ben jumped at the sound.

"You okay?" Janet was now wearing a pair of cutoff jeans and a light green T-shirt.

Ben nodded absently.

Janet had let down her hair and tucked it behind her ears. She put the cigarettes in the middle drawer of the dresser and hung the clothes she'd been wearing back in the closet. She replaced the lid on the can full of money and put it on the top shelf in the closet.

"Come on," Janet said, "let's go home."

"I *am* home."

"I know, I'm sorry, I mean . . . come back to . . . "

"No."

"What?"

"I'm staying here."

Janet looked worried. "I don't think that's a good idea."

Ben just stood there, rooted to the spot.

"Ben, you're sort of scaring me. Don't you think—"

"I'm not going to tell your parents."

"What?"

"I said, I'm not going to tell your parents you were smoking. Just let me stay here for a while. I'll come back later."

"You promise?"

Ben nodded.

"And you really won't tell on me?"

"No."

Janet straightened her shirt. "I owe you a favor, then. Anything you want."

There was a lingering moment of silence before Janet said, "We all miss her, you know."

Ben nodded.

"Don't stay too long, okay? A storm is coming."

Ben opened his mother's jewelry box and picked up the silver locket Janet had been wearing. His mom's name was Elaine Wilson, and the locket had a fancy *EW* engraved on the front. It was pretty. Ben had no idea where his mom had gotten it or why she'd never worn it. He tried to open the locket but it seemed to be sealed shut. He looked into the little mirror on his mom's dresser and put the locket around his neck anyway. The silver was smooth against his chest.

Janet had left the closet door open. Ben walked over and breathed in the familiar smell of his mom's clothing as he crawled inside. When he was little he loved hiding in here, behind her dresses, perched uncomfortably on her shoes. As his mom got ready for bed, she'd say, "I wish Ben were here to tuck me in," or "Too bad Ben isn't here to read this great book with me." He would hold his breath, trying not to laugh. Sometimes she'd call, "Ben, are you here?" and he would answer, "No!" At the last minute, she'd always say something like, "Well, I wonder where my slippers are," and she'd open the closet door and act surprised when she found Ben hiding inside. It had been a long time since they'd played that game.

Ben rested his head on his knees. He closed his good ear with a finger, blocking out the sound of the wind outside and the rain that had just begun to patter against the roof and the windows.

He thought about the coffee can sitting on the shelf above him. He crawled out, pulled over a chair, and took it down. There was a lot of money inside the can, maybe a few hundred dollars. Ben couldn't believe his mom had saved so much money. Did she have other secrets hidden in her room? What if his aunt and uncle sold the house before he found them?

He put the can back and felt around in her folded sweaters. Nothing. It felt strange, and wrong, to go through her things, but he couldn't stop. He climbed down and opened the drawers in the nightstand and in her dresser. He found endless bills and unreadable tax documents and articles ripped from magazines. There were files related to the library and a ton of papers he couldn't understand. Then, in the bottom right-hand dresser drawer, he found a plain cardboard envelope. He pulled it out and turned it over. There was no address or stamp. Carefully, he opened it.

Inside was something wrapped in tissue paper.

The paper wasn't taped down, so Ben pulled it off. He discovered a small blue book, its covers soft and creased with age. On the front, the title was stamped in black letters: WONDERSTRUCK.

He flipped through the pages. The book was about the history of museums. On the back it said: *Published by the American Museum of Natural History, New York, New York.*

Was this a present his mom was going to give him? Was she hiding it, waiting to surprise him?

Ben turned to the front of the book. A child had scribbled some pictures around the edges of one of the opening pages, little flowers and leaves. In the center was an adult's handwriting. In red ink, it read:

for Danny
Love, M

Ben wondered who Danny could have been, and who M was. The handwriting was old-fashioned so maybe the inscription had been written a hundred years ago. Maybe his mom had found it at the used bookshop in town. Or maybe someone had donated it to the library's annual book sale. Either way, it was Ben's now.

Sitting on the edge of the bed, he held the book as gently as he could. He hadn't read anything since the accident, but he turned a few pages in *Wonderstruck* and started reading.

Back in the year 1869, New York City had no museum of any kind, either for art or for natural history, such as were to be found in Boston, Philadelphia, Chicago, Washington, and in all the capital cities of Europe. Young Theodore Roosevelt built a small museum on the back porch of his house, and his father that same year enlisted in the movement to start the American Museum of Natural History.

But let us pause here and ask ourselves, What exactly is a museum? Is it a collection of acorns and leaves on a back porch, or is it a giant building costing tens of thousands of dollars, built to house the rarest and finest things on Earth?

"It's both!" Ben heard himself say out loud.

Of course the answer is both. A museum is a collection of objects, all carefully displayed to tell some kind of magnificent story.

Think of the endless examples of shells, rocks, bones, and gems on display in the grandest museums all around the world. These objects didn't appear out of nowhere. Someone, like young Teddy Roosevelt perhaps, collected, cataloged, and curated them.

Rain continued to cascade against the roof and windows, making a soft, distant, drumming sound as Ben read on.

A curator's job is an important one, for it is the curator who decides what belongs in the museum. The curator then must decide exactly how the objects will be displayed. In a way, anyone who collects things in the privacy of his own home is a curator. Simply choosing how to display your things, deciding what pictures to hang where, and in which order your books belong, places you in the same category as a museum curator.

Ben wondered if he was a curator. He had never stopped to think about *why* he collected things. It was just something he'd always liked to do. He thought about his wood box. Maybe it was a *museum* box. Maybe he was making a museum about Gunflint Lake.

There was a terrible crash of thunder. Ben rubbed the locket between his fingers, then turned a few pages ahead.

These early collections, centuries ago, were stored in pieces of furniture called Cabinets of Wonders. The cabinets were ornately carved, with dozens of tiny doors and drawers and hidden spaces filled with a nearly infinite variety of amazing items. Here, one could find everything from precious gems to unicorn horns, intricately carved ivory, and magical cups that could cure all poisons. Great and glorious works of art resided in these collections, side by side with the wonders of nature. Some collections grew beyond the confines of a single cabinet and took over entire rooms. The viewer was able to walk into one of these rooms and, as if reading a book, understand the wonder of the world just from the stories told by the collected objects and how they were displayed (see fig. 26).

Figure 26 showed an old drawing of the room

described above. Almost the entire room was covered in shelves, like his mom's library, except the shelves were much fancier. And it was filled with the strangest objects, some of which hung from the ceiling above. There were ornate glass jars, drawers of shells and bones, rows of birds, mysterious sea creatures, human heads and alligators, strangely shaped sculptures, and many things Ben couldn't identify at all.

In the center of the room was an intricately carved cabinet with a crown of seashells and coral on the top. Ben studied it in amazement.

The viewer was indeed supposed to feel a kind of "wonder" and awe while looking at everything laid out before him. If you've ever stood beneath the skeleton of a dinosaur, or gazed at a giant diamond, or come upon something beautiful in nature, a glowing red flower perhaps, growing alone from a cracked sidewalk, you know this feeling of wonder.

ARTCRAFT P

DAUG
S

STA

Li

May

"Oh
The st
he

No!

orm is

re!"

A brilliant bolt of lightning, white-hot and electric, came hurtling out of the sky, accompanied by another huge crash of thunder.

The lights went out.

Ben wanted to go back to his cousins' house now. He tucked the book into the back of his pants, pulled out his flashlight, and made his way to the kitchen.

He couldn't find any umbrellas, so he took one of his mom's winter coats from the hall closet and held it over his head for protection against the rain. Lightning kept flashing, momentarily illuminating the room like flashbulbs on a camera. Another crack of thunder shook the house, and Ben realized he had better wait out the storm here. Eighty-three steps could be very far in weather like this.

He put away his mom's coat and returned to her room. He crawled into the indentation in her bed and lay on his back. He propped the flashlight against his shoulder so it pointed upward and he held the book directly over him. Just as he was about to start reading again, something fluttered out of the book and landed on his chest. It was an old bookmark.

Ben sat up and inspected it. The bookmark was frayed at the edges and on it was a black-and-white drawing of a storefront, with books piled up in the window and spilling out of boxes and shelves on the sidewalk. A black cat sat listlessly near the door. The awning above the windows read KINCAID BOOKS. At the bottom were the store's address and phone number.

Ben turned the bookmark over. In black ink, someone had written:

February 1965. Elaine—This piece of me is for you. Please call or write. I'll be waiting. Love, Danny.

Beneath that were a phone number and an address in New York City.

"Where

find

from the

can we

elter

storm?"

Ben's whole life, as far as he knew, his mother had never had a boyfriend. She had friends on the lake and in town, and she stayed out late sometimes without telling Ben where she'd been, but she never brought anyone home with her, so he never asked. There was only Major Tom, but Ben knew he was just a fantasy. He stared at the date on the bookmark. It was from the year Ben had been born.

Things began to fall into place in his mind. If a man named Danny had known his mother the year he'd been born, and he'd signed a note with the words "*Love, Danny,*" was it possible that he could have been his mom's boyfriend? And if he *was* a boyfriend, could he, by any chance, have been Ben's father? In an instant, it all seemed possible. He'd ask his aunt in the morning if she knew anything.

Ben looked again at the address on the bookmark. His mind reeled with the idea that his father might live in New York City. And then he thought about all the money in the rainy-day fund.

Ben rubbed his forehead as his imagination took over. Maybe his mom had been planning something much bigger than a trip to Duluth. Could she have wanted to take him to *New York City,* to introduce him, for the first time, to his father?

Ben had been holding his breath, and he exhaled. What was he thinking? Even if Danny *was* an old boyfriend of his mom's, there was no proof that he was Ben's father.

Ben pulled on the chain around his neck again and absently ran his fingernail along the edge of the locket. To his surprise, he felt a click as the locket opened.

He expected to see a little photo of his mom, but instead there was a tiny black-and-white photo of a *man*. He had a mustache and sideburns and big dark eyes that looked familiar to Ben somehow.

The photograph had dislodged slightly from the locket. Ben carefully removed it. On the back was a single word: *Daniel*.

The photo trembled in Ben's hand.

He turned it over again and pressed it back into the locket. He stared into Daniel's eyes. Now he knew why they looked so familiar. They were *Ben's* eyes.

There *was* proof!

His father wasn't Major Tom, lost forever among the stars. His father was *Daniel* and he lived in New York City.

Ben looked at the phone number on the bookmark. All he had to do was call.

He moved toward the blue phone sitting on the nightstand. He read the phone number several times.

Outside, the storm grew worse. Still shaking, Ben picked up the receiver and held it to his good ear. He hesitated, then dialed the number.

He slid the bookmark back between the pages of the
book.

The phone was ringing.

The

An Artcraft P

End

ures Production

SOUND
NEW
"TALKIE"
WORLD ELECTRIC
EQUIPMENT
LISTEN TO THE MOVIES
CLOSED
SOUN

EXPRE

100% all

SEE+

ALL

PAV

IENCE

talking

HEAR

YOUR

RITE

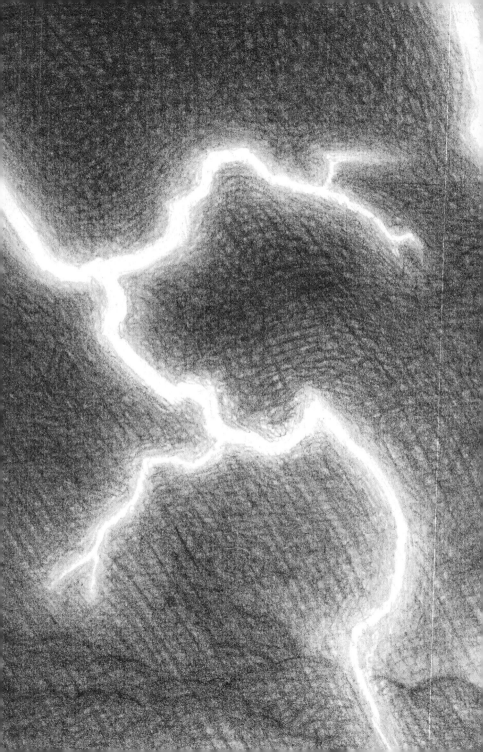

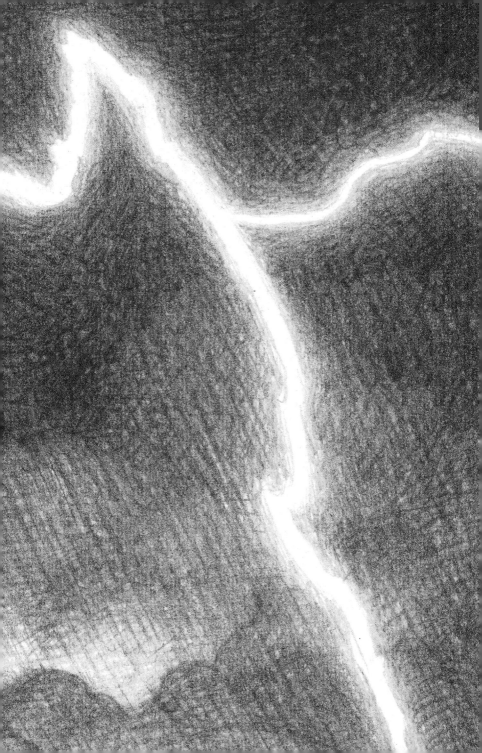

When Ben opened his eyes, he was lying on the floor, staring at the ceiling.

Something smelled terrible and burnt. Thankfully, the rain had stopped and everything was silent and peaceful. He could go back to his cousins' house now.

He wanted to get up but he felt so tired. The bed, the nightstand, and the dresser seemed terribly far away, as if Ben were looking at them through the wrong end of his telescope.

In the distance, he saw the blue telephone. It was off the hook and seemed to be smoldering.

Then, through the windows, he saw something that seemed impossible. He saw *rain,* still pouring down from the sky, streaking hard against the glass. He saw lightning flash without thunder.

How odd, he thought. The storm *hadn't* stopped. Such quiet rain. It had been so loud before. Where had all the noise gone?

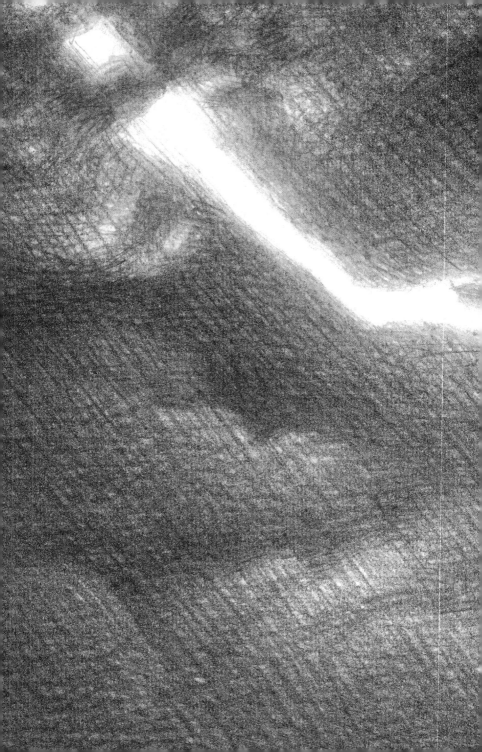

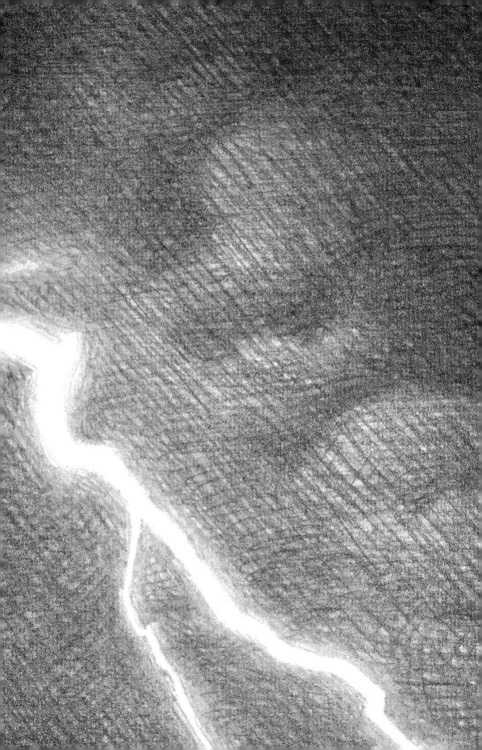

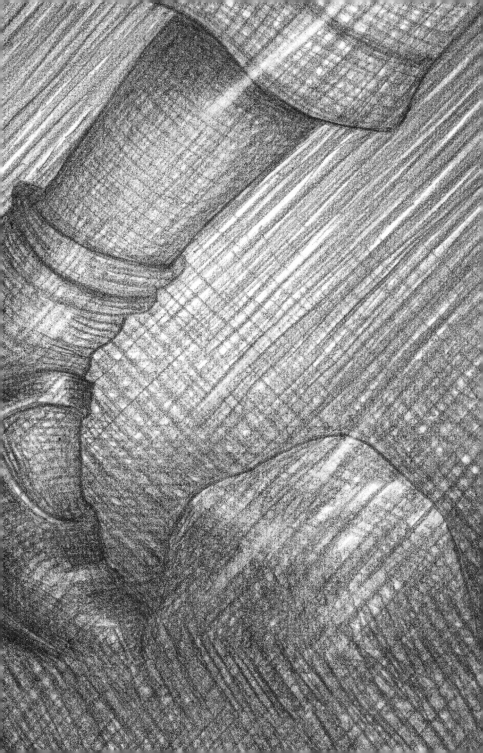

Ben tried to yell for help but no sound came out. He looked around. His mother's room had turned cold and white. Harsh electric lights stared down from the ceiling. Machines and tubes surrounded him. This wasn't his mother's room.

A woman dressed in white arrived. She was wearing a little white cap, and a stethoscope hung around her neck. A name tag clipped to her uniform read LINDA. Her eyes were kind.

A nurse? Why did he need a nurse? Was this a hospital? How had he gotten here?

Ben stared at Linda's mouth, which was moving, but she wasn't saying any words. Why wasn't she speaking?

He tried to get up to go to the bathroom, but Linda stopped him. Her mouth was moving silently again. She put her finger to her lips as if she was saying, "Shhhhh." He wanted to scream at her to speak up, to tell him what he was doing here, but he was too tired and his head hurt too much. He let her ease him back onto the pillow and he closed his eyes. He must have cried out, because another nurse came and gave him some medicine. Linda placed her fingers by the side of his head, next to his good ear, and made a snapping motion. Why wasn't there any sound? Linda took out a chart and wrote something down.

Ben's eyelids felt heavy so he let them close. Maybe he was just dreaming.

Was it days later or only a few minutes when his aunt Jenny appeared? Her eyes were red and watery. She sat on the bed and stroked his hair. He thought he could smell the food she'd been cooking at the lodge as she ran her fingers down his cheek just like his mom used to. He watched her lips move. He looked at the nurses talking to each other. His head felt like it was full of leaves. He opened his mouth to say he couldn't hear but nothing came out.

The nurse handed Aunt Jenny a piece of paper and a pen. She wrote a note and handed it to Ben.

"I know you can't hear. Don't try to talk. Just lie still."

Ben's head throbbed. How did she know what he'd been thinking?

"You've had an accident. You're going to be okay, but you were hit by lightning."

Aunt Jenny crossed out two of the words and rewrote them.

". . . ~~you were~~ your house was hit by lightning. The lightning traveled through the wires and into the phone, which you were holding to your ear."

Ben rubbed his good ear, or what had *been* his good ear. Hit by lightning? What had he been doing in his house? Why had he been holding the phone? He tried to remember but all he saw was a silver locket. Instinctively, Ben's hand went to his neck, but the locket was gone.

"Janet found you in your mom's room this morning. I'm so sorry, Ben. You have been through too much."

Ben tried to sit up to say something, but his aunt gently eased him back and brushed the hair from his eyes. She blew her nose and continued to write.

"The doctors need to run more tests. We're going to transfer you to the Duluth Children's Hospital tomorrow."

Duluth? Ben was going to Duluth? Hadn't he once wanted to go there?

He looked at his aunt and had a vision of a glowing yellow curtain. Then the seashell turtle appeared, and an old blue book, and then all the images blurred together.

Ben's head and body ached so much that he had to close his eyes again. He must have cried out, because the nurses came with more medicine and adjusted his IV. Slowly, slowly, the pain began to slip away and the silence swallowed him whole.

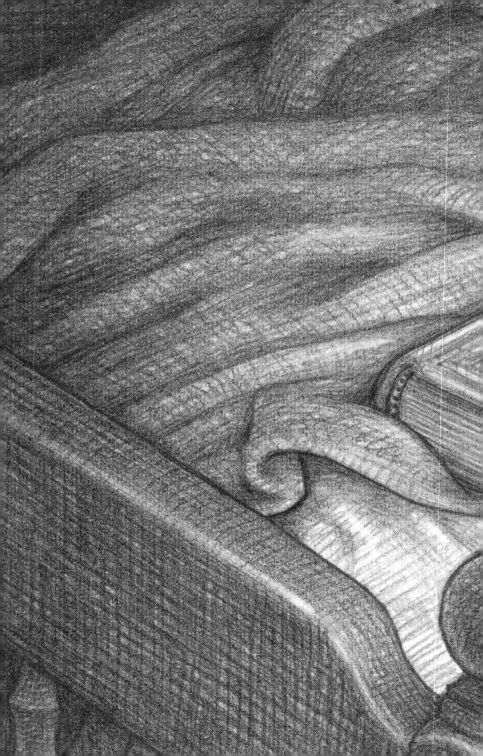

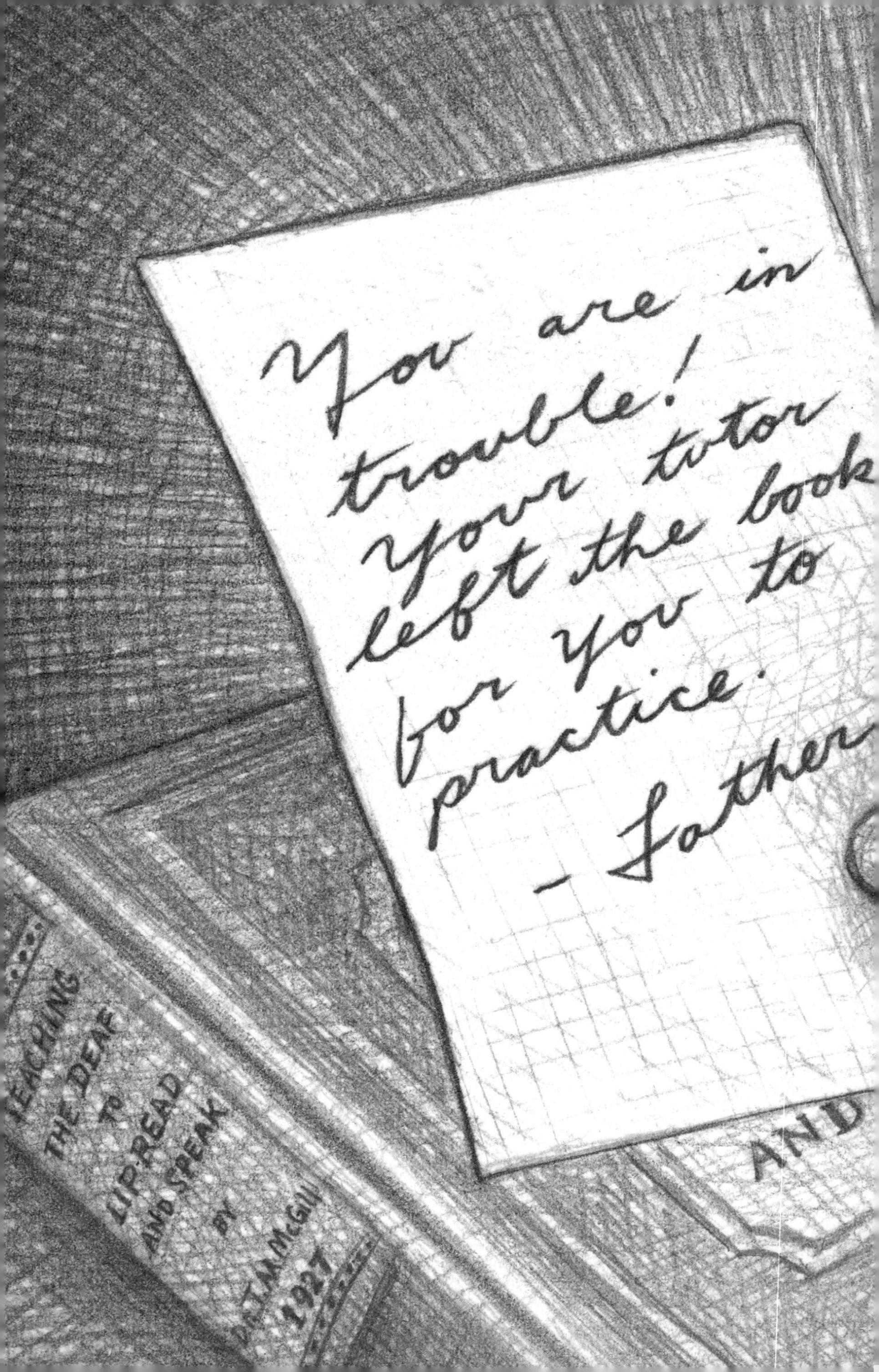
You are in trouble! Your tutor left the book for you to practice.
– Father
TEACHING THE DEAF TO LIP-READ AND SPEAK
BY
McGill
1927
AND

TEACHING THE DEAF TO LIP-READ AND SPEAK

INTRODUCTION

In this volume we will discuss how best to teach the deaf child to communicate. We must remember that spoken language brings a child more closely into contact with the world. A deaf person who cannot lip-read or speak has only one means of communication with the world— pencil and pad. The more speech a deaf child has, the larger his circle of friends.

In the uneducated deaf-mute we see the mind confined within a prison. He knows nothing of the touching power of the human voice. But with much work the deaf can be helped to communicate with the hearing world. Even Miss Helen Keller said her own education in speech and lip-reading brought her from isolation to "friendship, companionship [and] knowledge."

So let us begin our work.

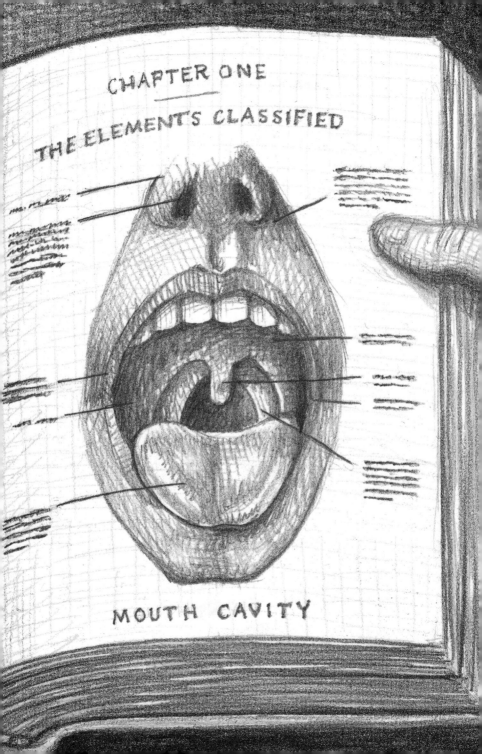

Ben heard the wind and the clacking of the boats in the water, the musical chirp of birdcalls, footsteps crunching through the snow, and the distant sound of human voices. Fragments of his life rose up to the surface only to be pulled back under. He struggled to keep his head above the water.

"And I'm floating in a most peculiar way. And the stars look very different today."

A room covered in ornate shelves and strange objects built itself around Ben. Teddy Roosevelt was there waving from a porch. And his mother's bed was waiting just for him. He curled up in the indentation. A bookmark floated through the air and landed on his chest.

Ben smelled cigarette smoke blowing in beneath the door. He heard howling as his bed rose up and drifted into space. He was an alien, circling the North Star as Major Tom waved good-bye.

"For here am I sitting in a tin can, far above the world."

And there, a million miles below, he saw a wolf.

It was beautiful.

And it was dangerous.

And it was running through the streets of New York City.

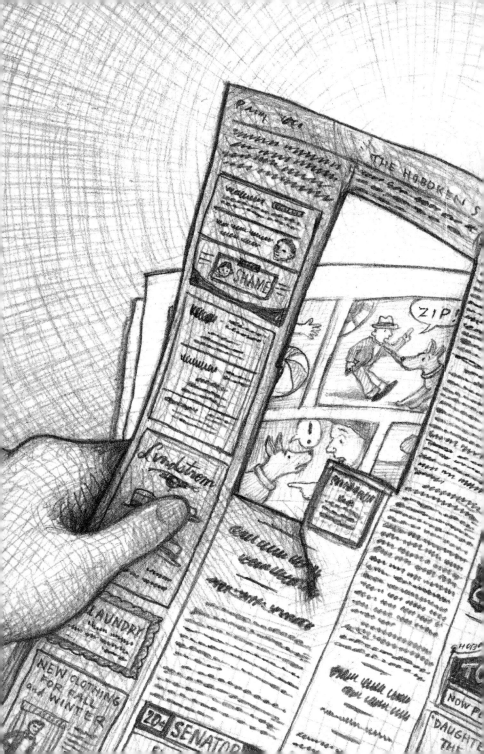

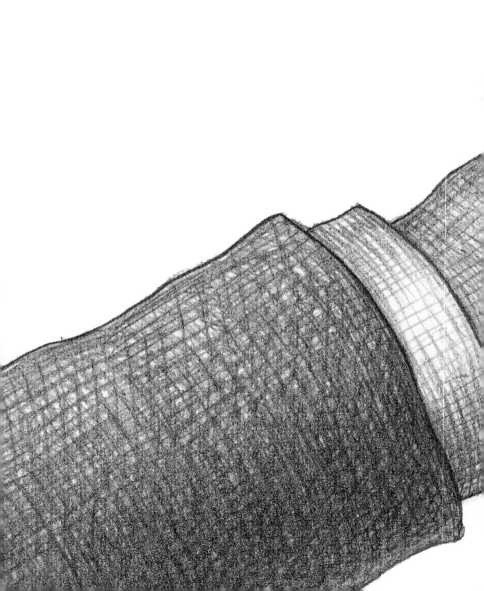

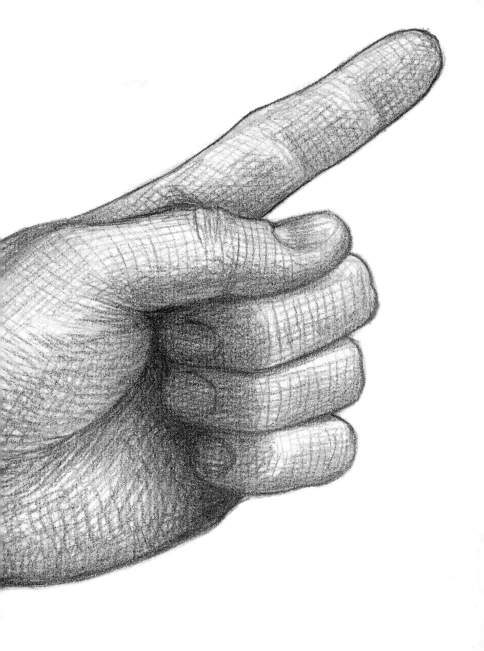

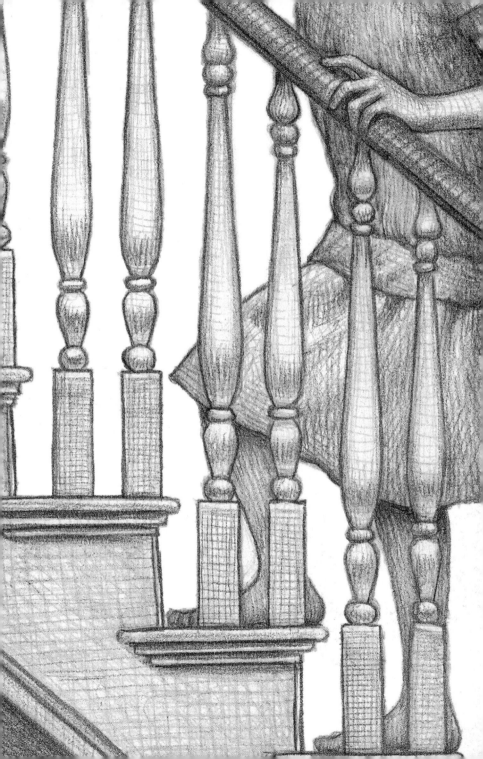

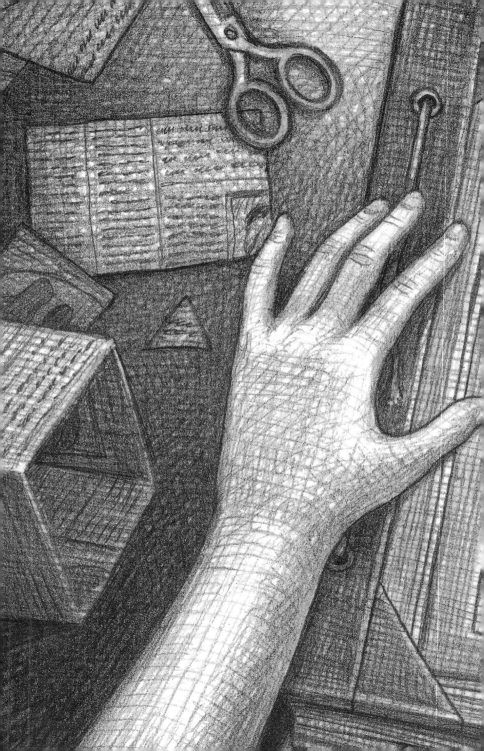

MAYHEW GLOWS

MISS MAYHEW
TELLS US ALL

LILLIAN MAYHEW
AS ANTIGONE

TICKET

LILLIAN MAYHEW
IS ENGAGED

LILLIAN MAYHEW MARRIES DOCTOR

W—

Rings

LIAN
MAYHEW
in The
DOOMED

Lillian Mayhew

STARRING IN

LOVE NOTES

PART TWO

Ben felt the heat of someone's skin against his cheek. He opened his eyes and found himself leaning against a tall young man asleep in the seat next to him.

The bus shook and rattled. It seemed as if he'd been on the road for months, but it couldn't have been more than a day or two.

Ben squeezed the suitcase that lay on the floor between his feet. The clasps were broken but it managed to stay shut. He was hungry and his head still rumbled, the way it had ever since the lightning strike a few weeks earlier.

As the world sped by outside the dirty bus window, Ben rubbed the smooth silver locket between his fingers.

He was happy to have it around his neck again. He pulled it back and forth along the thin chain, and wished he'd remembered to leave behind a note.

Ben didn't want to fall asleep again, but he soon found himself dreaming that the wolves were chasing him all the way from Gunflint Lake. When he awoke, he was out of breath, as if he'd been running for miles. His head throbbed.

Ben realized the bus was no longer moving. The young man next to him was gone, as was everyone else. There was a strange stillness all around him, like time had stopped.

He pressed his face against the window. For a moment Ben thought that he might still be dreaming.

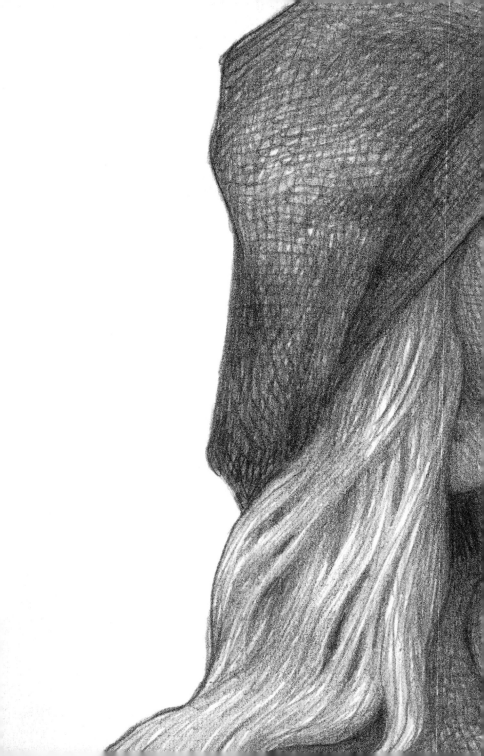

Was Ben really here? Holding his suitcase, he stepped off the bus into the rank, hot station. His legs felt wobbly, as if he were standing in a canoe. How long had he been on the bus?

A clock on the wall said 9:30. But there were no windows in the station, so he didn't know if it was 9:30 in the morning or in the evening.

He followed the crowd through the vast gray and red spaces of the station. Everything was lit by dingy fluorescent bulbs, half of which were broken or flickering. They made Ben's eyes hurt. The filthy floors stretched on forever. Along the walls, ragged people lay curled up on unfolded cardboard boxes. It was so quiet.

And then Ben remembered that he still couldn't hear. The doctors had said his hearing might return. They ran so many tests in the hospital and discovered the lightning had damaged his eardrum. Ben looked down at all the silent shoes in the station and up at all the silent mouths. What would life be like if his hearing never came back?

He followed the rush of people around corners and down escalators until they all came to a set of big glass doors leading outside, into the bright light of morning.

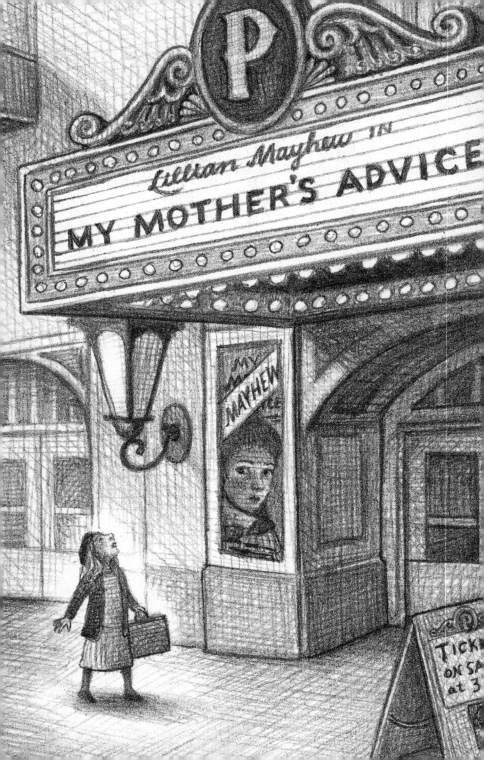

STAGE
DOOR ➤

Quiet Please

REHEARSA

IN PROGRESS

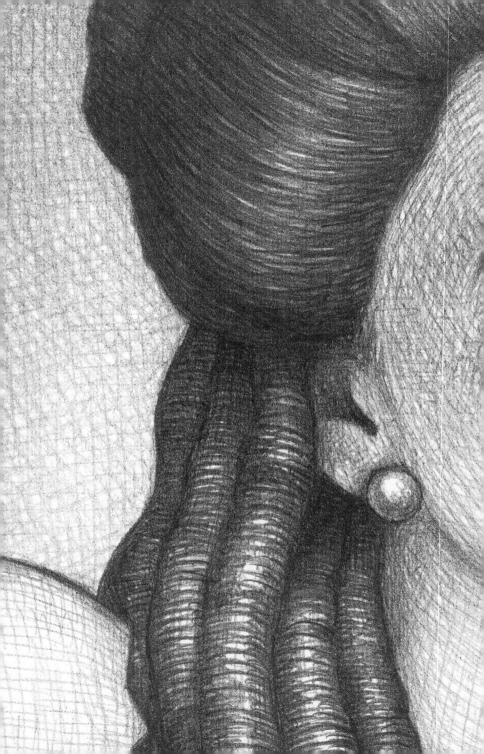

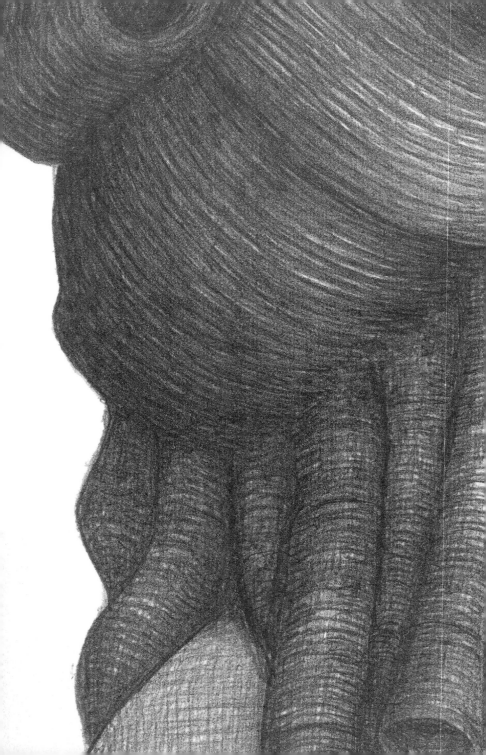

The street was a riot of cars and flashing signs and people. Buildings climbed toward the sky on either side of the street the way the trees back home surrounded Ben's house. Dirty cars and yellow taxis paraded by. Smells he couldn't place bombarded him.

From the sidewalks, newspapers flashed headlines like "Heat wave!" "Murder!" "Scandal!" and "Kidnapping!" Spray-painted words covered broken windows. Rows of movie theaters advertised films he'd never heard of and didn't want to see.

Ben looked around in astonishment. Taking in all the colors and smells and movements, he felt like he'd fallen over the edge of a waterfall. He was sure he had never seen this many people in his entire life on Gunflint Lake. Everyone everywhere seemed to be a different color, as if the cover of his social studies textbook had come to life around him.

A man in a tattered army jacket and battered pants lay along the curb, propped up on an elbow, his eyes closed. A little dog with skinny legs was between his feet. Beside them was a tin can with a few coins in it. Ben reached into his pocket, bent down, and added all of his change. The city seemed to swirl and explode around them, and even though Ben was sure it had to be the loudest place on earth, the man and his dog slept through it.

Ben tried to imagine the honking, screaming, screeching soundtrack, but to him it unfolded noiselessly, like a scary movie with the sound turned off. All he could hear in his mind was David Bowie singing about Major Tom.

Shoelaces and buttons and tiny rocks gathered in the cracks of the sidewalk. When Ben bent over to pick up a little souvenir for his museum box, a woman with tiny shorts and a giant hairdo rolled by on skates and accidentally knocked him over.

After he got awkwardly back on his feet, Ben pocketed the pebble he was grasping in his hand and walked to a hot dog cart on the corner of Forty-second Street and Eighth Avenue. He had no more change, so he set down his suitcase between his legs and pulled out the cash from his back pocket.

As he stood there counting the bills, a hand darted out from behind him.

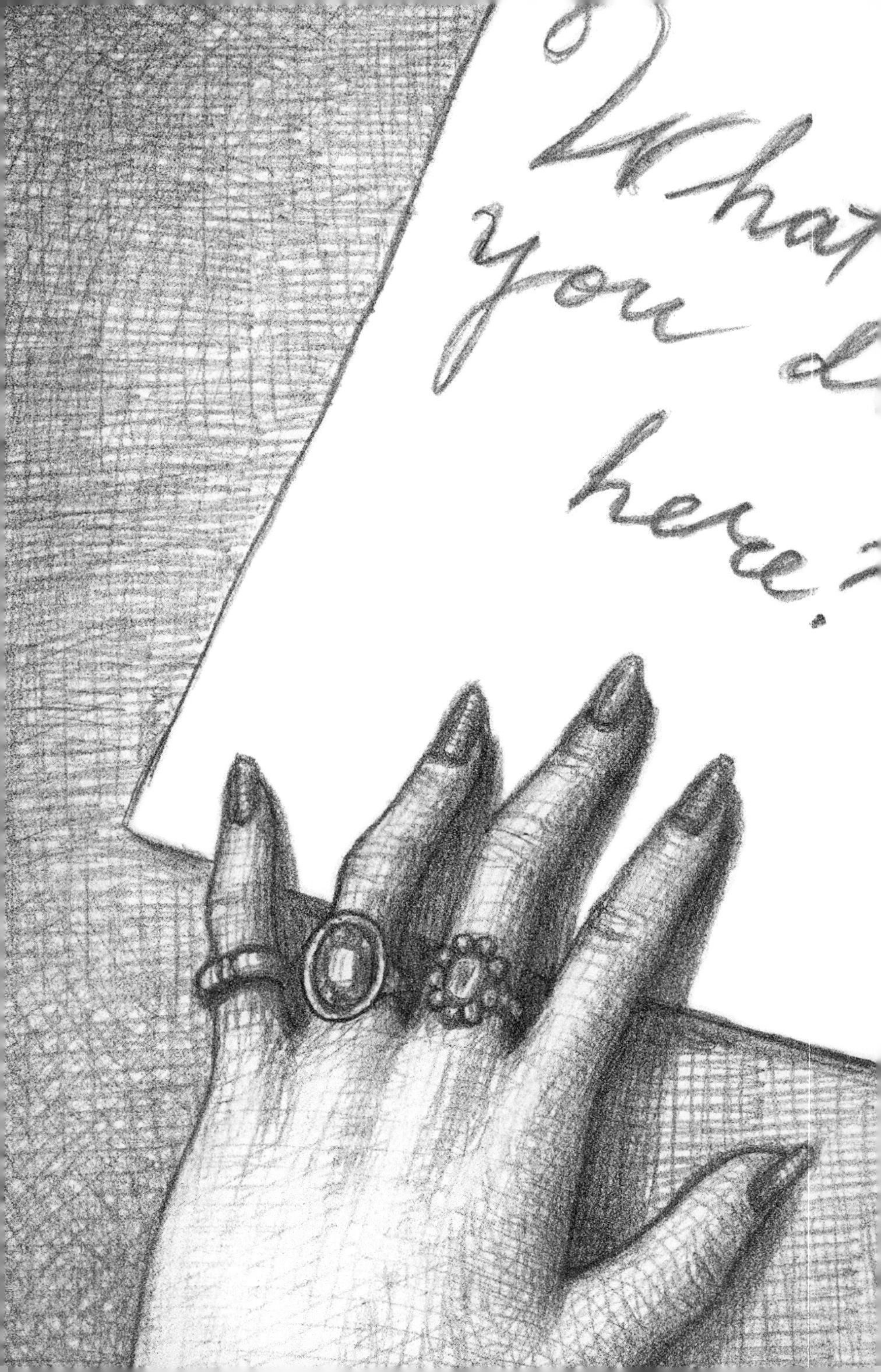
you
here

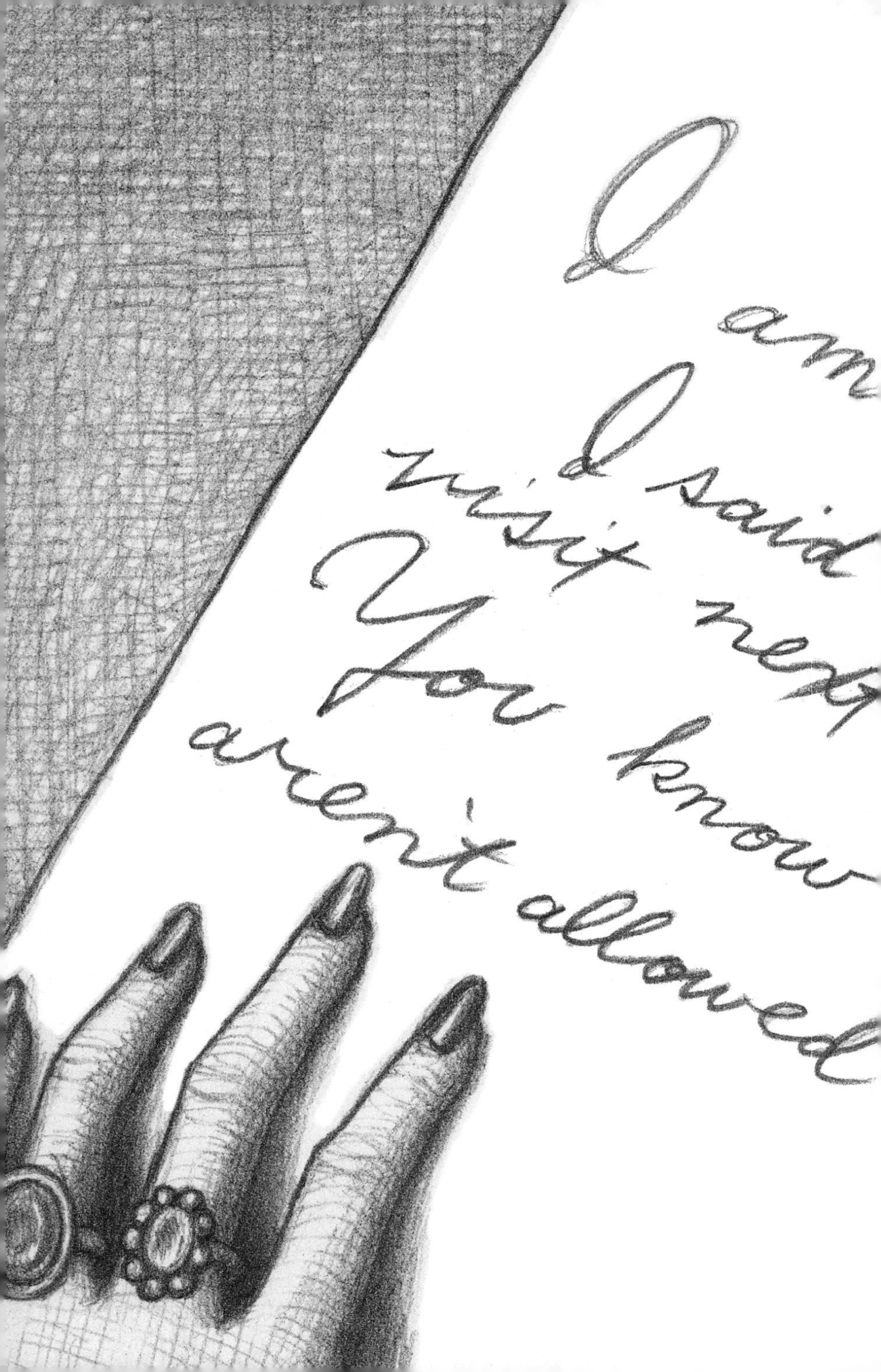
I am
I said
visit next
You know
aren't allowed

please make

We're
enough!
dangerous
girl to be
alone. You
be hit by a car
kidnapped.!

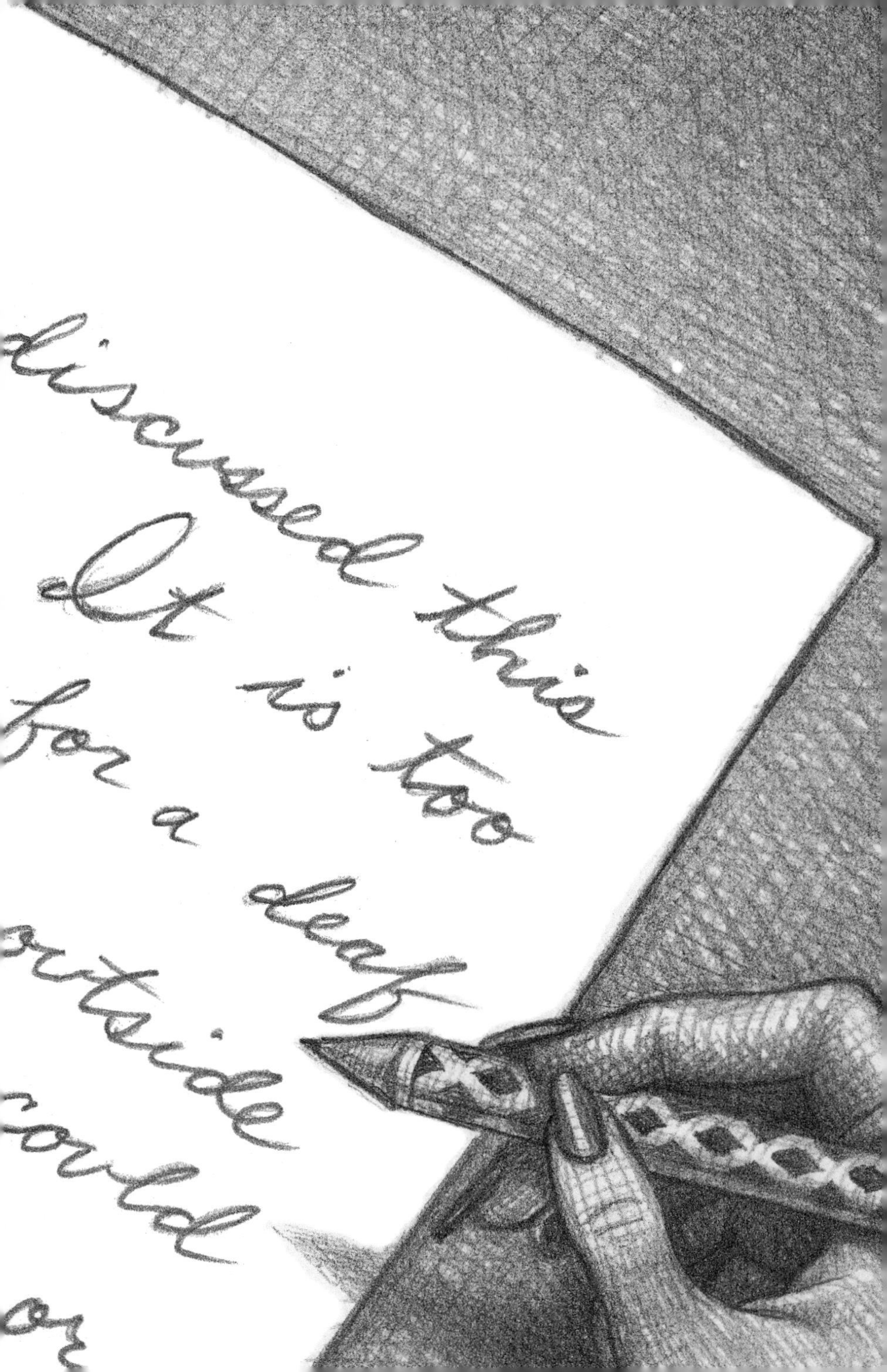

discussed this
It is too
for a deaf
outside
could
or

So
any

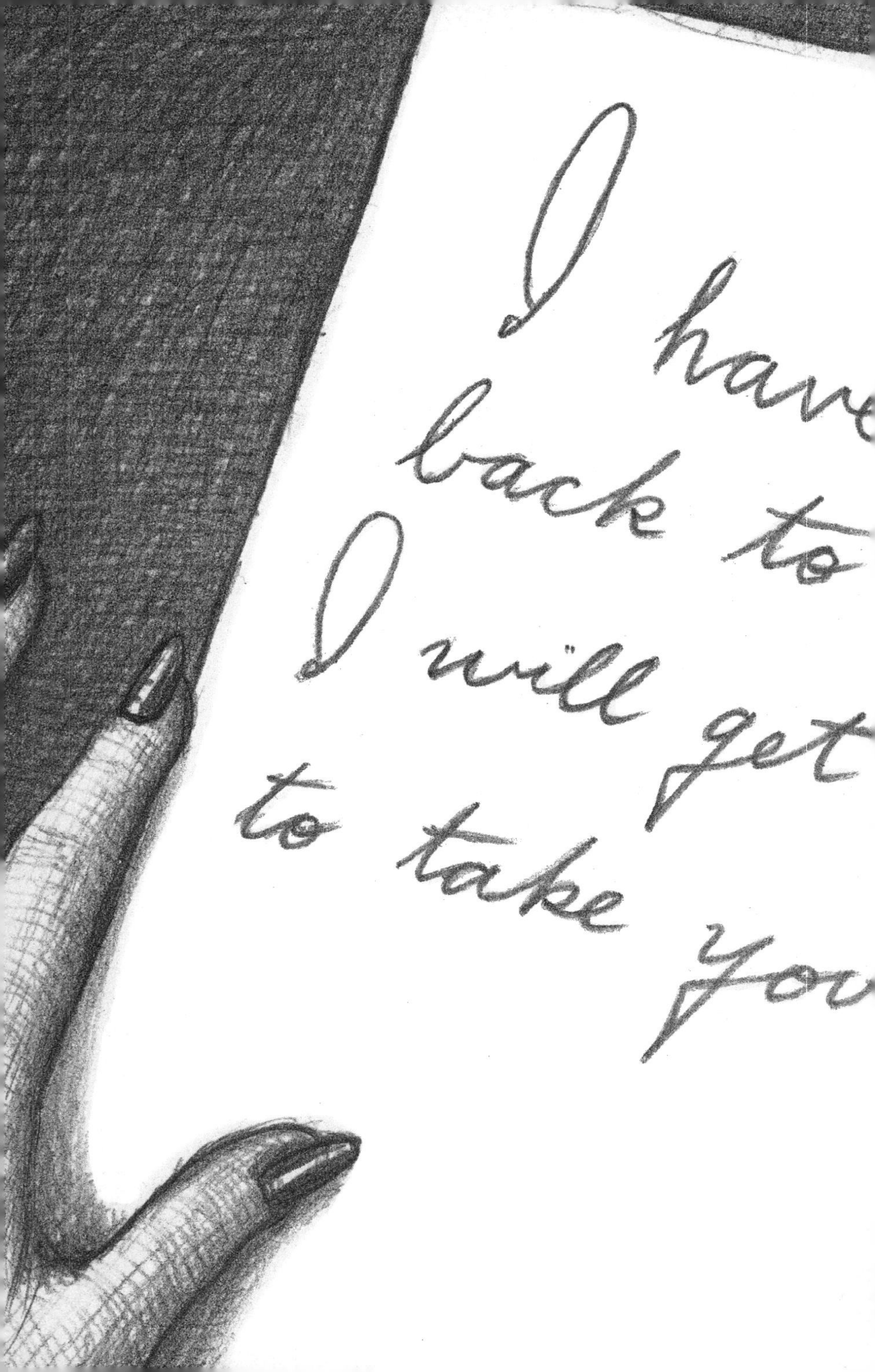
I have
back to
I will get
to take you

Ben was knocked to the ground again. He watched a large figure in purple sweatpants and a white T-shirt disappear into the crowd. He looked down at his empty hands and felt stupid for taking out his money and counting it on the street. He'd read books about New York and seen it on TV and in movies. He knew how dangerous the city was supposed to be.

He stood up again and pulled the bookmark from his pocket. He read his father's address, looked up the street, and squinted. He saw Forty-third Street, so he walked in the direction of the higher numbers, along Eighth Avenue. He was glad the streets were in numerical order. It would be easy to follow them up to Seventy-fourth Street.

He was halfway there when a taxi appeared from nowhere and brushed Ben's leg. A hand grabbed his shirt and yanked him back onto the sidewalk to safety. It belonged to a woman with a blue kerchief tied around pink curlers in her hair. She shook a finger in Ben's face.

Rattled, Ben kept walking. Soon he arrived at a gigantic traffic circle. Trying to look in every direction at once made Ben dizzy. Which way was he supposed to go? He held the bookmark out to a woman walking a fat, brown dog and pointed to his father's address. The woman paused just long enough to read it. She moved her mouth and gestured toward the road that bordered a huge park. Ben dodged the cars as he ran through the traffic circle. Soon he was walking beneath the swaying green trees that hung over a wall separating the park from the sidewalk. There were fewer people here than near the bus station, but it was still crowded compared to Gunflint Lake.

At last he arrived at Seventy-fourth Street. There was only one way to turn, so he made a left and walked past rows and rows of brown and tan buildings, all with stairs leading up to doors on the second floor. A dirty white cat scuttled across the sidewalk into a pile of garbage bags. Ben checked the address on the bookmark again. He looked up and realized he was standing in front of his father's building.

Ben's heart beat wildly as he climbed the steps and studied the brass panel of doorbells. Next to each button was a little piece of paper with a name on it. Most of the paper had disintegrated, though, so the names were unreadable.

Ben put down his suitcase, wiped the sweat from his forehead, and looked once more at the bookmark before returning it to his pocket. He pressed the button for 3B. He kept pressing it with one finger, unsure if it was connecting, while his other hand rubbed the smooth silver locket around his neck.

After a few minutes a small woman in a thin blue nightgown opened the door. She had gray hair and brown skin shiny with perspiration, and she didn't look happy. She was already talking when the door opened. Ben just stared at her mouth.

"I'm looking for Daniel," he interrupted, still finding it strange to use his voice when he couldn't hear himself. "He's my father." Ben opened the locket and showed the woman the photograph.

The woman stared at the photo, then at Ben. A look of displeasure crossed her face. She kept talking, using her hands sometimes to punctuate a point. Ben could not figure out what she was trying to tell him.

Back home, even when his family and the hospital

staff had written things down for him, they still talked a lot, and Ben realized that he had to do a huge amount of guesswork to piece together a conversation.

He closed the locket, put it inside his shirt, and tried a different question.

"Does Daniel live in 3B?"

The answer this time was clear: no.

Ben felt faint. Why had it never occurred to him that his dad might not live here anymore?

Feeling desperate, he said, "Do you know where he lives now?"

The woman seemed to laugh and then said something else, and Ben could tell she'd never heard of Daniel. He kept staring at her mouth. He thought he recognized the word *mother* on her lips. Was she asking where his mother was?

Ben pointed to a big white car parked nearby. A woman was sitting behind the wheel. "That's my mom," he said.

The woman at the door sneered and said something Ben was sure wasn't nice. Then she shut the door in his face.

Tears stung his eyes, and the street seemed to turn upside down.

How stupid he was for thinking it would be that

simple. He sank down onto the top step and buried his head in his hands.

After a few minutes, Ben opened the locket and stared into his dad's dark eyes. "Where are you?" he asked. "What do I do now?" He didn't even know his dad's last name.

At a loss for where to go, Ben pulled the bookmark from his pocket again. His dad's handwriting was fading where it ran through the creases.

He turned it over and looked at the drawing of Kincaid's and the black cat and all those books. He had no other clues, so he decided to walk to the bookstore. If his dad once lived in this neighborhood, maybe the people at Kincaid's would remember him. It was a long shot, but he didn't know where else to turn.

Ben continued uptown. After a few blocks, he stopped at a red stone building set back a little bit from the road. It was surrounded by trees and seemed larger than any of the other buildings nearby. The name of the building fluttered on a banner hung between two columns.

It looked like a castle from a fairy tale.

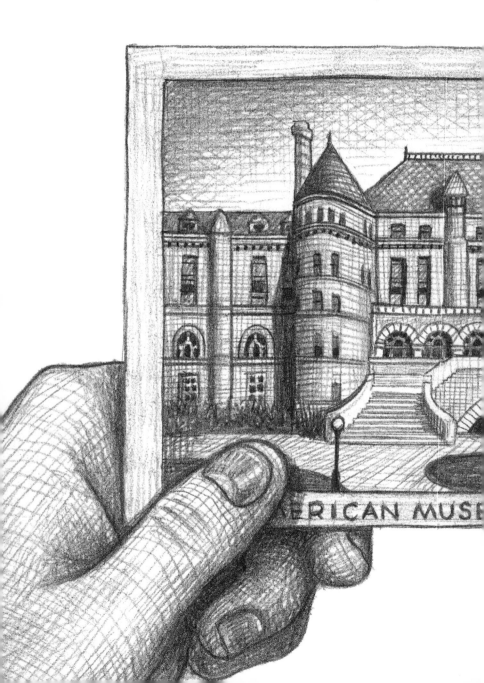

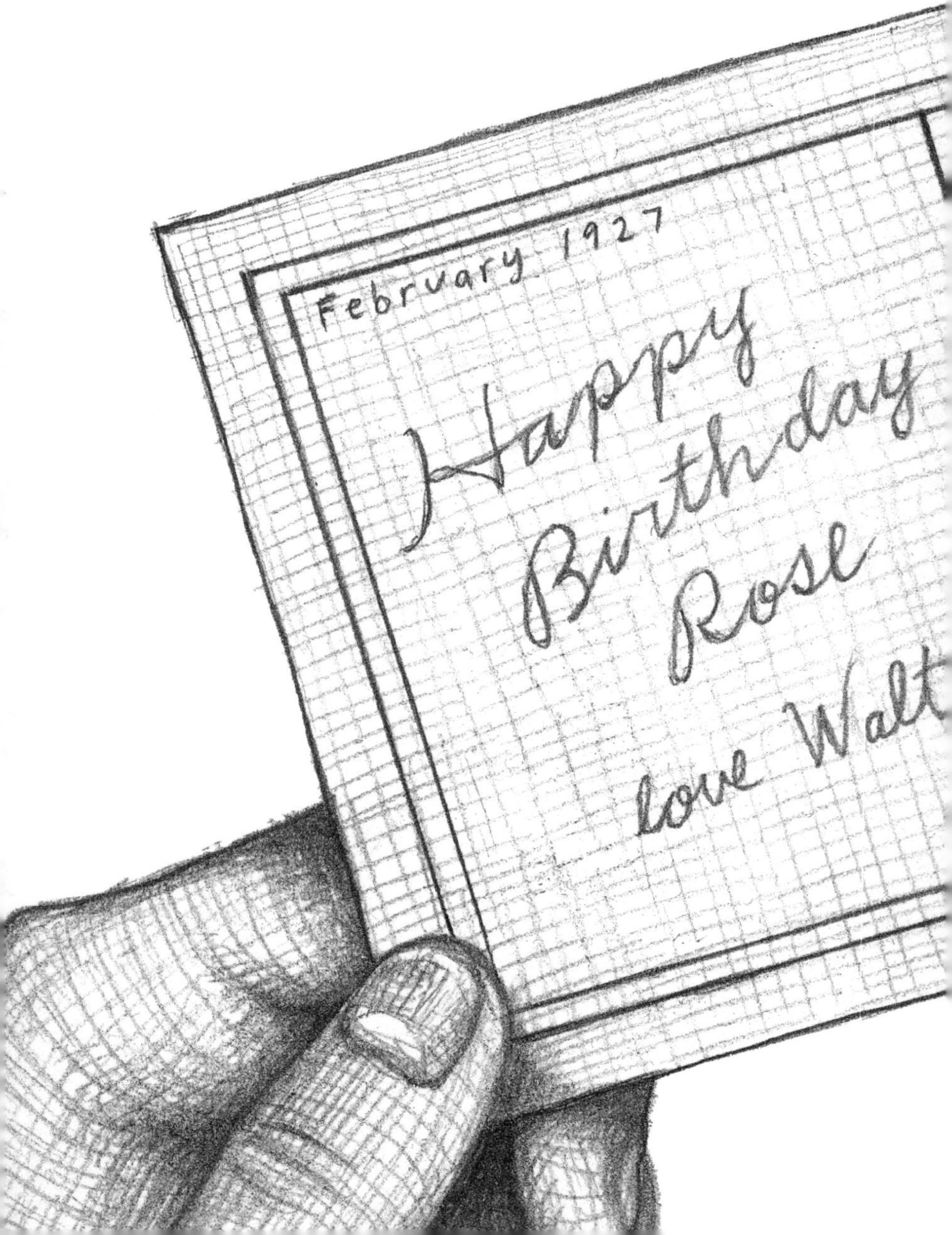
February 1927
Happy
Birthday
Rose
love Walt

Miss Rose Kincaid
168 River Street
Hoboken, N. J.

Ben studied the museum in awe. The steps, the giant green statue of a man on horseback, the columns and windows . . . it was magnificent. If only his mom were here with him, walking beside him, her arm on his shoulder. Did she know his dad had moved, or would she have been surprised as well? Even if they hadn't been able to find Ben's dad, he and his mom could have gone into the museum together.

Ben prayed that someone in the bookstore would remember his father. By the time he arrived at the address on the bookmark, his T-shirt was completely soaked through with sweat.

Cigarette butts and bits of newspaper gathered in dirty piles on the ground in front of the store. He looked up at the storefront window. There was no black cat or boxes of books. There was no bookstore at all, just a padlock running through a metal grate that was pulled down over a broken glass window. Plywood sheets were nailed up in pieces behind the grate. Remnants of a sign that read KIN   BO K hung at an angle from a single nail.

Ben pressed his eye against a hole in the plywood and felt his stomach turn. Except for a few rows of fallen shelves, some pipes leaning at odd angles, and a couple of overturned cardboard boxes, the store was empty.

Now what would he do?

As he stared in disbelief, a boy about his age appeared from nowhere, startling him. The boy had long, curly, black hair and wore a striped T-shirt. He had a Polaroid camera around his neck and a knapsack on his back. He was moving his lips and pointing down the block. What did he want? A man standing nearby waved impatiently to the boy.

Ben's head roared. He gathered up his things and ran. The heat was unbearable and his skin burned in the sun, but he kept going until he was back at the museum. He bounded up the stone steps, past the statue. At the top, he tripped and the clasps on his suitcase finally gave way. Everything he owned tumbled out onto the stairs.

Ben bit down on his lip to keep from crying again. As he bent over to pick up his things, a shadow fell across him. He glanced upward and saw the curly-haired boy in the striped T-shirt looking down at him, his mouth moving. The boy handed Ben *Wonderstruck,* which he must have picked up off the stairs. Ben took the book, placed it in the suitcase, and snapped it shut. Then he rushed past the boy and pushed through the revolving doors.

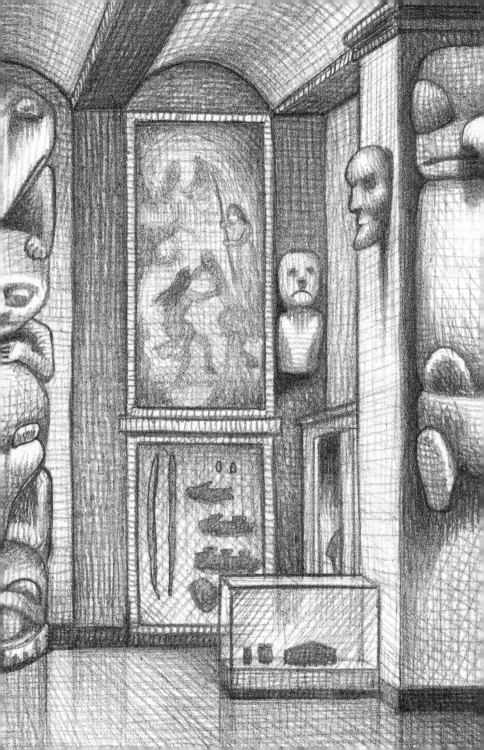

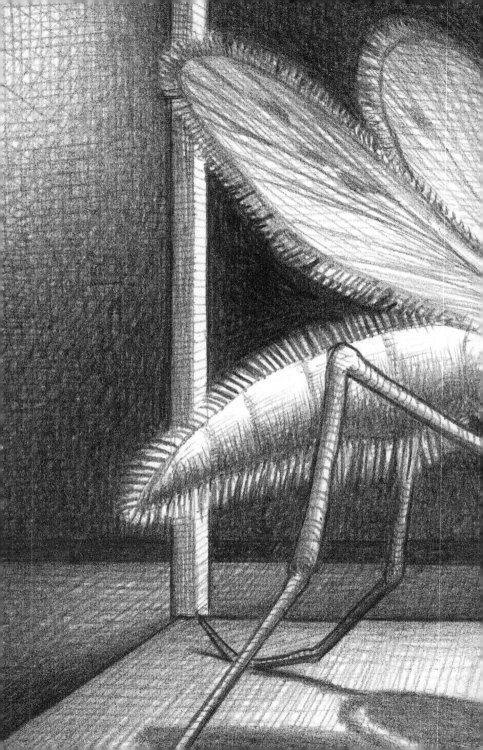

The air inside the museum was cool. Light filtered in from high above. It reminded Ben of the church down the road from his mom's library. The walls were covered with warmly colored murals teeming with people and animals and plants. There were long quotations from Theodore Roosevelt painted on the wall as well. *It is hard to fail, but it is worse never to have tried to succeed.* Ben wasn't sure he agreed, but he thought his mom would have liked that. She would have put it on the refrigerator.

Ben had no money for admission, so he waited for someone to ask the guard a question, then he snuck swiftly under the ropes. He found a bathroom and took a long drink from the faucet. He washed his arms and face. The cold water felt good against his skin. He looked at himself in the mirror, and for a second it was like staring at a stranger. With the water and dirt dripping down his exhausted face, he really did look like an alien.

As he dried himself off, he noticed a discarded map of the museum next to the sink. He unfolded it and read the names of the halls: Meteorites, Gems and Minerals, Man in Africa, Northwest Coast Indians, Biology of Birds, Small Mammals, Earth History. Like his mom's library, the entire universe was here, organized and waiting.

Outside the bathroom was a small café. On one of the tables, someone had left a tray with the remains of a sandwich and half a carton of milk. Ben made sure no one was looking, then he inhaled the sandwich and drank the milk. He hadn't realized how hungry he'd been.

He followed signs to the elevator and rode to the top floor. With the map in his hands, he easily found the dinosaur skeletons, which rose above him like ancient roller coasters. He wandered beneath flocks of birds hanging from the ceiling, past Komodo dragons with forked tongues sticking out at him, and two giant, unmoving tortoises protecting their eggs. "Look, Mom, turtles!" he said to himself.

Continuing onward, like a boy lost in a castle, Ben walked through gigantic hallways and down marble staircases. He discovered a herd of elephants standing on a raised platform as if they were posing for a photograph. In the Hall of Ocean Life, a whale hovered in midair like a blue zeppelin. Sharks mounted to the walls looked ready to eat him, their deadly white mouths wide open.

All through the museum, Ben marveled at the life-size dioramas cut like windows into the dark walls. The dioramas looked out into endless vistas, blazing sunsets, snow-capped mountains, and high fields of grass. Each one was filled with animals that seemed to be frozen in time. They turned their heads, or sat waiting on rocks, or walked toward a stream, and then paused, midbreath, forever.

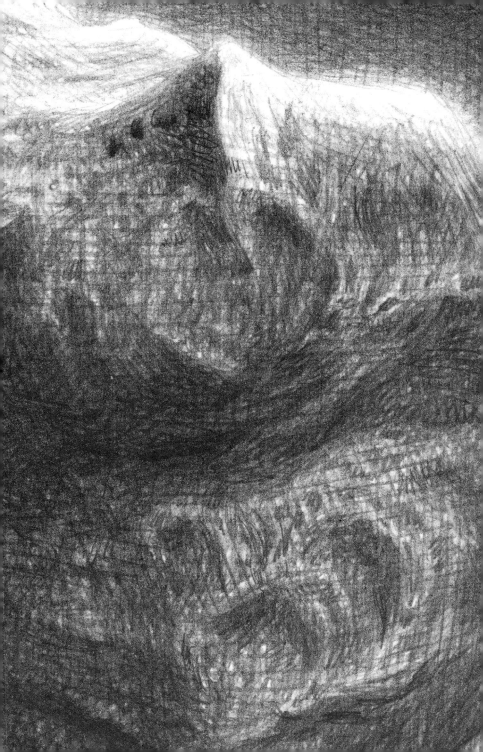

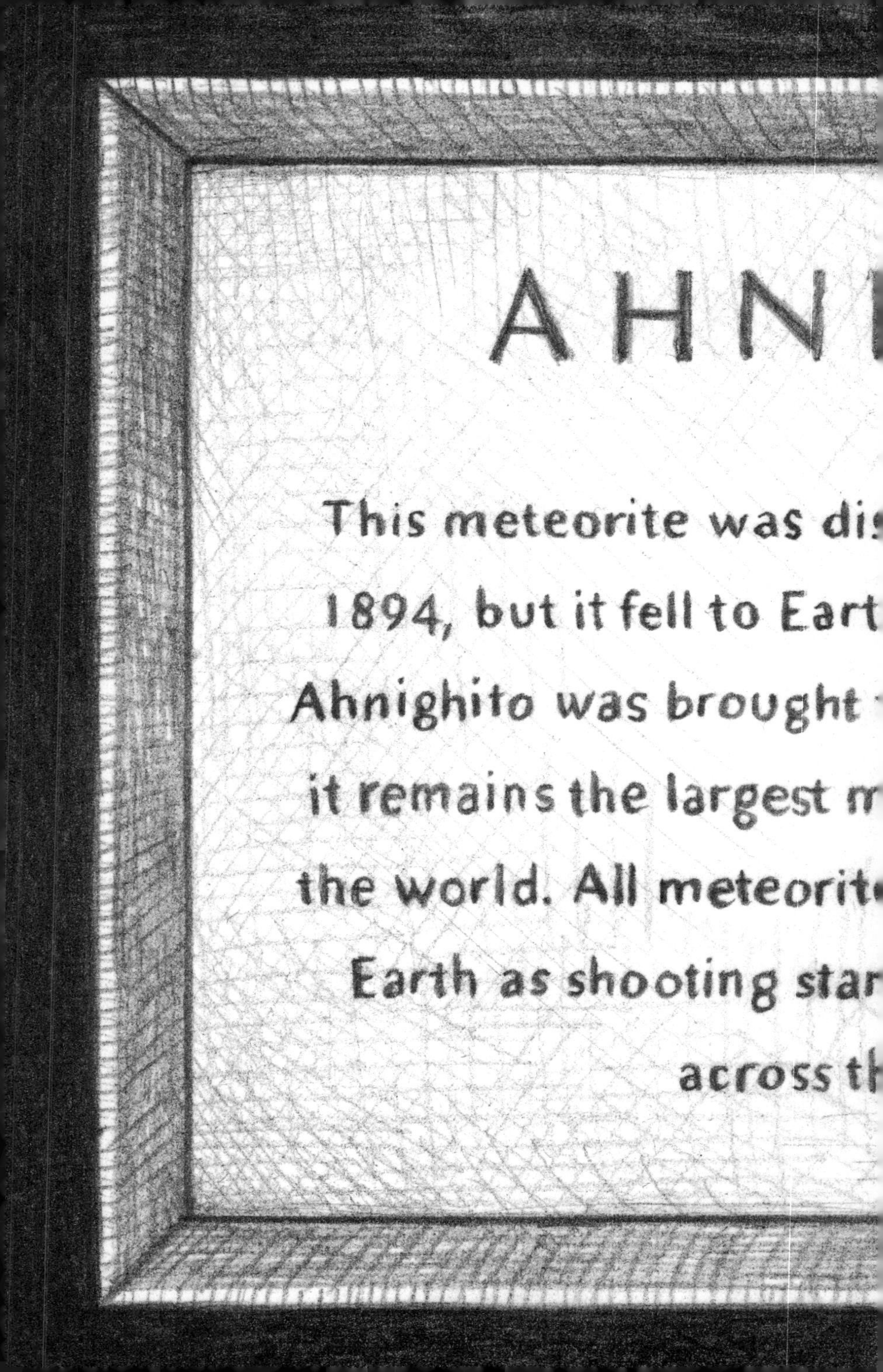

AHNI

This meteorite was dis

1894, but it fell to Eart

Ahnighito was brought

it remains the largest m

the world. All meteorit

Earth as shooting star

across th

GHITO

...vered in Greenland in
...ousands of years earlier.
...e museum in 1902, and
...orite in any museum in
...egin their journeys to
...treaks of white light
...ight sky.

d. All m

s shooti

ac

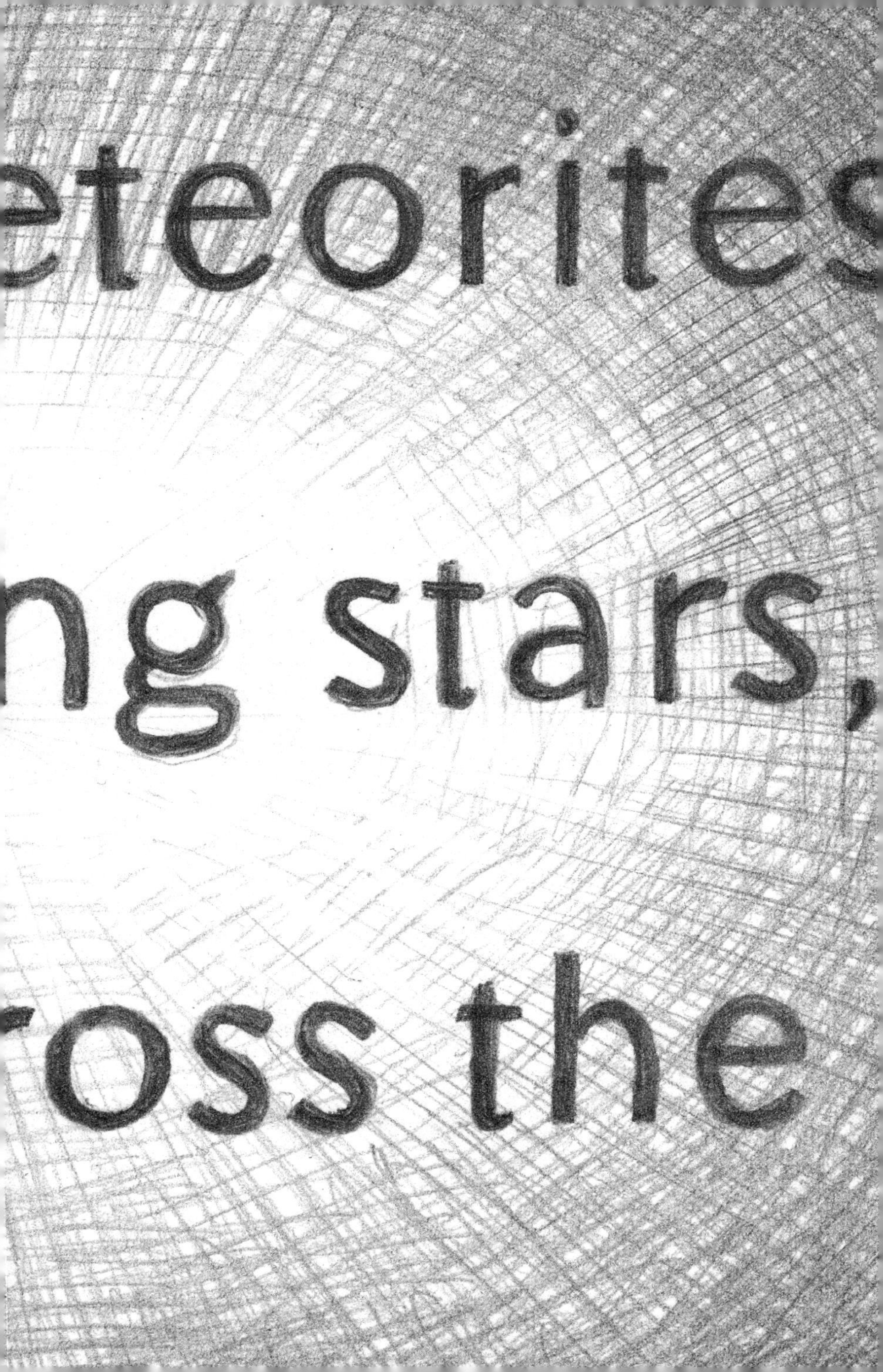

eteorites

ng stars,

ross the

Ben soon stepped into a dark, round space that seemed as if it had been built around the main object in the middle of the room. There, beneath the glow of a spotlight, was a gigantic black meteorite about the size of a car.

Ben ran his hand along the shiny, undulating surface.

It was smooth to the touch. He read the nearby sign and thought about the meteorite his mom had described to him, the one that had created Gunflint Lake two billion years ago. Had it been bigger than this one? And if a meteorite was the same as a shooting star, could you still make a wish even after it had fallen to Earth?

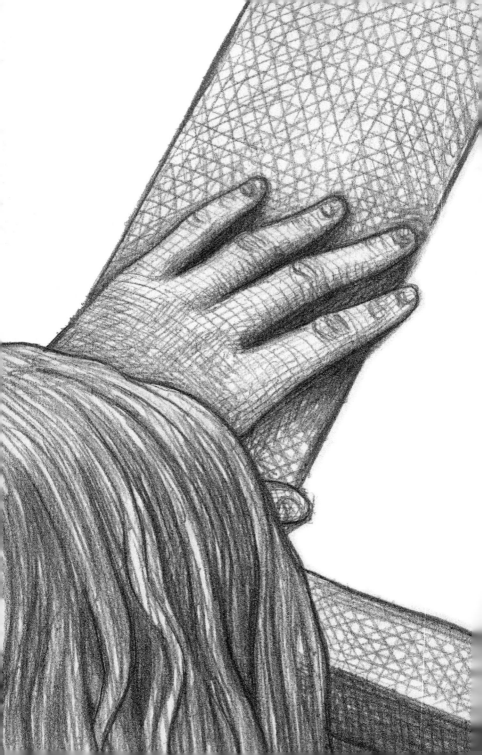

I wish
I Belonged
Somewhere.

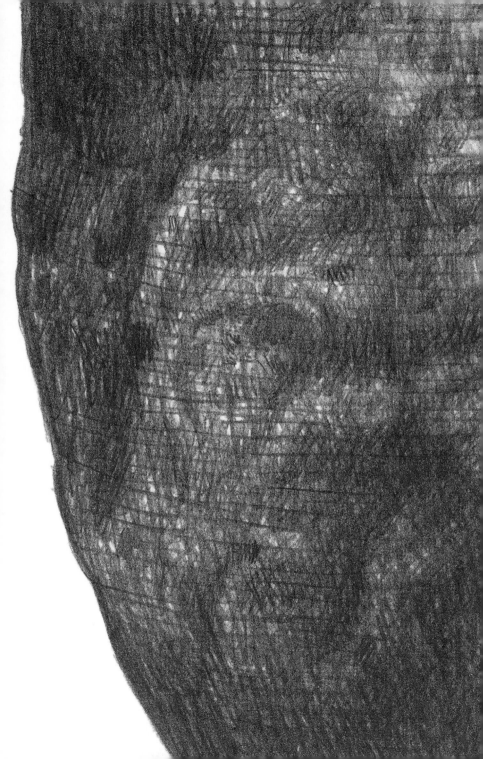

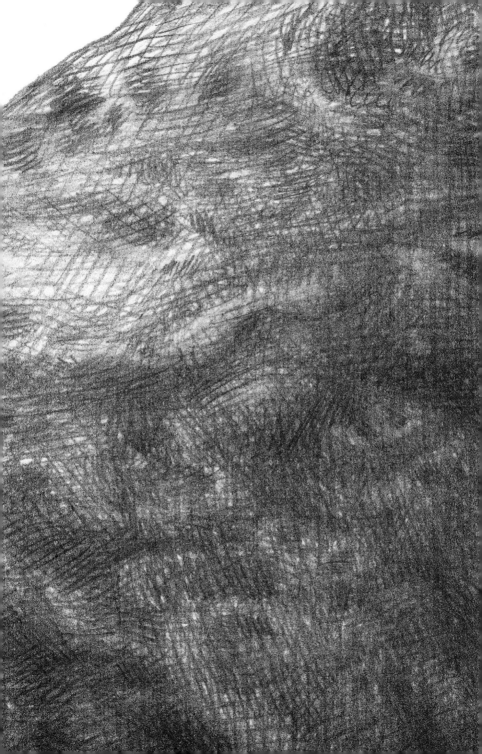

Ben pressed his hands against the meteorite. He loved how solid it was. He placed his suitcase on the ground, rested his cheek on the smooth surface, and closed his eyes. He made another wish.

When Ben opened his eyes and looked up, he noticed a mirror on the ceiling reflecting coins on top of Ahnighito. Amid the silver change, he saw a small piece of folded paper. Before he could reach for it, he was jerked backward, away from the meteorite. He turned and found himself facing an angry guard who was gripping his shoulders and obviously yelling at him. Just as Ben was about to apologize, someone darted past, behind the guard, and Ben tried to shake himself free but couldn't. He tried to read the guard's lips. He thought he was asking where Ben's parents were.

"My parents told me to meet them in the Hall of Ocean Life in ten minutes."

The guard shook his head, said something else, and then looked toward the Hall of Gems and Minerals, where there seemed to be a problem. He said one last thing to Ben before walking away.

Carefully, Ben balanced on top of his suitcase, reached up, and grabbed the note. He unfolded it. In green ink, it read: *What's inside the box?*

How long had the note been sitting up there? Ben

wondered. He reread it and thought about the museum box in his suitcase. Had he put it back when everything spilled out on the steps? He couldn't remember. He opened his suitcase and dug through his clothes.

The box wasn't there!

Turning the note over, Ben discovered a little hand-drawn plan of the museum's first floor, also in green ink. Running through the whole thing was a long dotted line that twisted through hallways and ended, like a treasure map, with an X.

Ben followed it room by room until he came to a narrow corridor lined with dioramas he hadn't passed before. The X on the map was in front of the fifth one.

Looking at the diorama, Ben felt the hair on the back of his neck stand up. His suitcase dropped from his hand.

He was staring into the shimmering lights of the aurora borealis cascading across a painted night sky. Beneath the blue light of an unseen moon, two wolves were running across a snowy landscape, heading right for Ben. A terrible shiver rippled through him.

It was as if someone had cut out the dream from his brain and put it behind glass.

Ben read the name of the diorama written in raised gold letters.

WOLF (CANIS LUPUS), GUNFLINT LAKE, MINNESOTA.

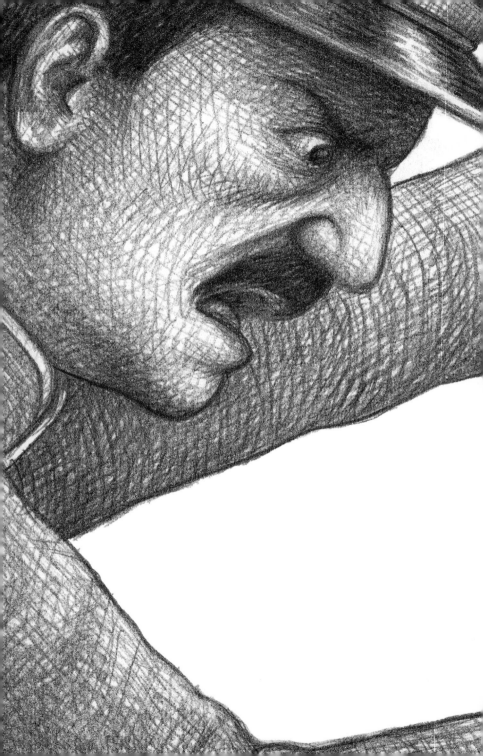

Ben felt his knees buckle. He stumbled backward until he was sitting on the floor against the opposite wall.

How was this possible? The wolves couldn't be here . . . but they were. He was staring at them with his own eyes.

Someone ran toward Ben and helped him stand up. He was so disoriented that it took him a minute to realize it was the boy with the curly hair.

A family with two little kids stepped around Ben's suitcase, which was still in the middle of the floor. The curly-haired boy ran over to get it, and Ben could see him apologize to the woman. As he returned the suitcase to Ben, his mouth was moving. Ben watched his lips, then said, "Thank you." He straightened himself up and rubbed his face with his hands.

The boy smiled a lopsided grin. He took the green knapsack off his shoulders and unzipped it. He pulled out the museum box and handed it to Ben, who hugged it to his chest. The boy was still talking, and Ben could tell he was supposed to answer a question he had asked, but he had no idea what the question was.

Ben interrupted. "Why did you pick this diorama to meet me at?"

Then he watched helplessly as the boy answered. Ben stared at his lips and his pointing hands, trying desperately to figure out what he was saying. Before the lightning strike, every now and then he would cover his good ear and try to lip-read. He was never able to do it, unless the words were very simple. Ben kept staring at the boy's mouth. He repeated his question.

The boy cocked his head and squinted at Ben. His mouth moved some more, and then he pointed to the diorama.

Ben nodded.

With exaggerated slowness, the boy's hand extended forward and pulled the museum box from Ben. He pointed to the engraving of the wolf on the lid, then back to the wolves in the diorama.

Of course! The wolves on the box had given the boy the idea to meet him here!

An old woman with long white hair walked up to the diorama and stood right next to the boys. She smiled kindly in their direction, without really looking at them, then stared into the moonlit diorama. Ben and the boy waited for her to leave, but she just stood there, looking at the wolves, and the trees, and the curtain of lights in the painted sky.

The boy pulled Ben away from the glass to let the old woman have her time with the wolves. He led Ben down the hall to the mountain goat diorama.

Ben closed his eyes for a moment and leaned against the wall. When he opened them again, the boy's mouth was moving, and his hand was beside Ben's head, making a snapping motion, just as the nurse had done in the hospital. The boy reached into a pocket and pulled out a little spiral-bound notebook and a green pen.

He wrote something and handed the notebook to Ben, who read the words: *"Are you deaf?"*

Reluctantly, Ben nodded.

"No wonder you ignored everything I said!"

Ben shrugged.

Motioning toward the old woman, the boy wrote, *"She's here all the time."* Then he pointed to himself and wrote, *"Jamie."*

"I'm Ben."

Jamie started making strange shapes with the fingers of his right hand. When Ben didn't respond, Jamie wrote, *"Don't you know sign language? I learned the alphabet in school."*

Ben shook his head.

"Why not?"

Ben touched his ear. "It's only been a month," he said.

"What happened?" Jamie asked.

Ben read his lips. "Lightning," he answered.

"Lightning?"

Ben nodded.

"I thought lightning killed you," Jamie wrote.

Ben raised his eyebrows as if to say, "I guess not," and Jamie looked as though he understood.

Jamie gestured toward Ben's suitcase. *"Runaway?"*

Again, Ben nodded. He saw Jamie mouth the word "Wow," then Jamie wrote, *"From where?"*

Before Ben could answer, the old woman walked past them, out of the hall.

The boys returned to the wolves. Ben stared into their shiny glass eyes, mesmerized, until Jamie tapped him on the shoulder and placed his fingers next to the words *From where?*

Ben pointed to the golden letters on the diorama that spelled out GUNFLINT LAKE.

Jamie laughed.

Ben pointed again, staring hard at Jamie.

The boy's eyes went wide. He put his hands on Ben's shoulders and moved him so he was standing with his back to the glass. Then Jamie backed up, lifted his camera, and snapped a picture.

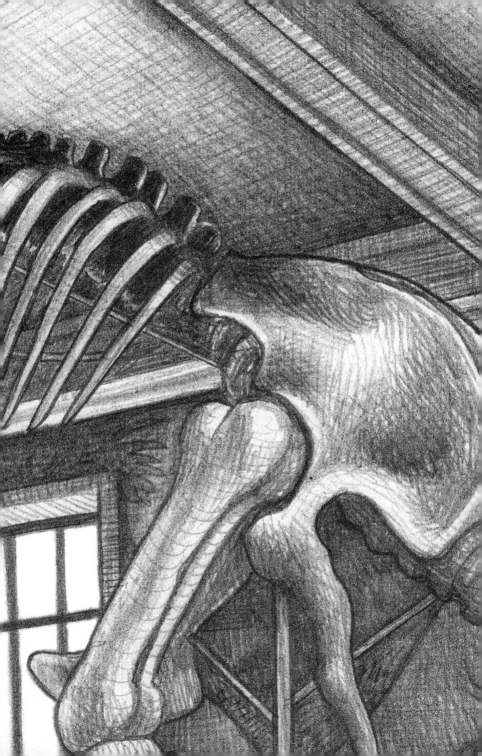

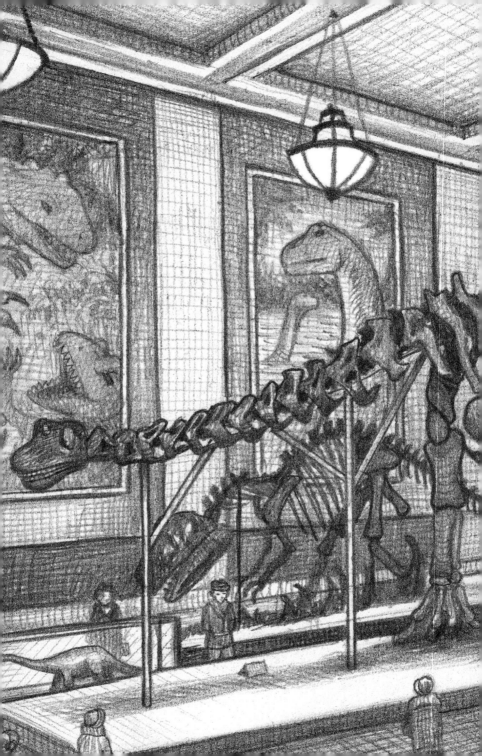

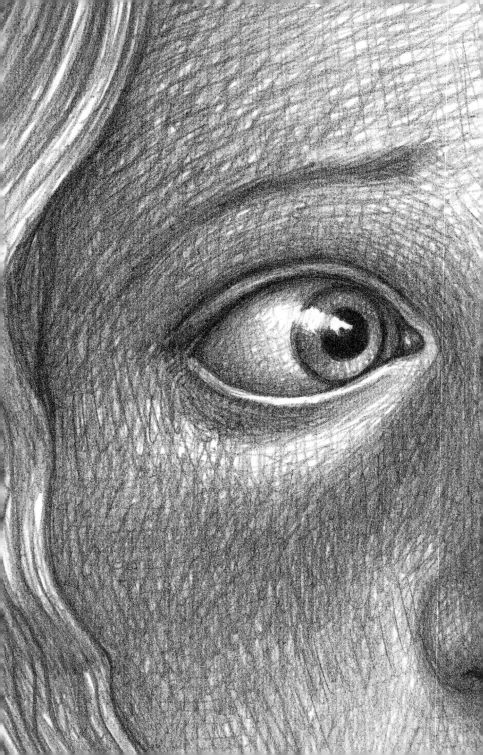

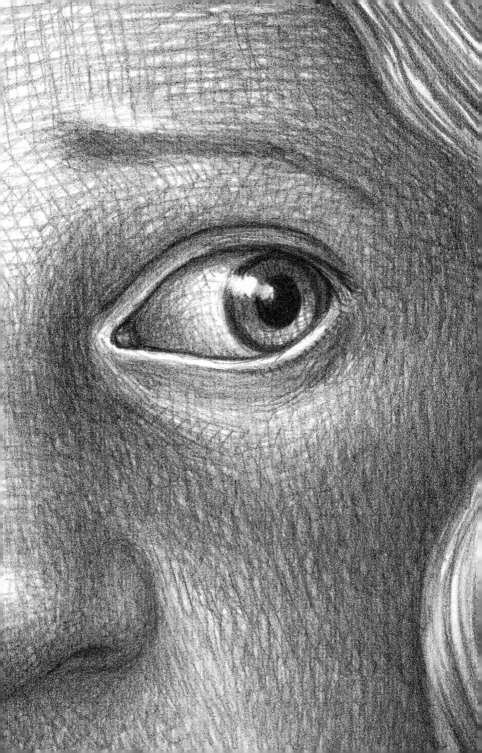

The bright white flash blinded Ben for a second. He shuddered, remembering the lightning. When his eyes adjusted, Jamie was smiling his crooked smile at him, holding the photograph he'd just snapped, a gray square with a white border, which had slid out from a thin slot in the front of the camera. Ben knew it would develop by itself in the next few minutes, but Jamie shoved it in his pocket before the image was done.

"Why did you do it?" Jamie wrote in his notebook.

"Do what?"

Jamie mimed "running away" by moving two of his fingers like little legs.

Ben didn't know how to answer. He just knelt down and returned the museum box to his suitcase. Jamie motioned with his hand, and Ben knew he was supposed to follow him. He didn't want to leave the wolves, but he was exhausted and didn't know what else to do. He wished he could just sleep.

They walked through long hallways and up staircases until they came to a door that read KEEP OUT. Jamie pulled a set of keys from his pocket, shook them happily in front of Ben's face, then quickly opened the door. Ben stared into the dim light on the other side of the door, afraid for a moment to enter.

Jamie must have seen Ben hesitate because he took

him by the arm, and the two boys slipped inside.

Dirty plastic tarps covered the windows, so the light was dusty and gray. The room was filled with boxes and old books, which lined the shelves all the way to the ceiling. Paper spilled out everywhere and water leaked down a wall. A pile of furniture was jumbled together in a far corner. Everything had a thick layer of dust.

Ben looked around and said, "What is this place?"

Jamie wrote, *"My secret room."*

"No. What *was* this place?"

Jamie shrugged. *"Storage?"*

Ben studied the towering piles of boxes and papers. It reminded him of the moldy archive room at his mom's library, with its shelves of ancient noncirculating newspapers and magazines. Jamie pulled one of the boxes off the shelves and removed a fur blanket. The tag on the back identified it as an object from a caveman display in 1947. He shook it out. With his foot, Jamie cleared away the dust and dirt from an area of the floor toward the back of the room. Beneath the grime was a checkerboard pattern, although most of the paint had faded. Ben was tired, but he was sure he'd seen the pattern before. Maybe it was in the bus station or somewhere else in the museum.

Jamie laid the caveman blanket on the ground. He removed a flashlight from another box, handed it to Ben, and the two boys sat down. The blanket smelled a little musty, but it was soft and comfortable.

Jamie reached into his knapsack again and pulled out a sandwich. He handed half to Ben, who ate it quickly even though it was tuna fish, which he didn't like very much.

"Thanks," he said between bites.

Ben felt a little better after eating, but he still just wanted to sleep. Maybe he could rest here for a while, on this musty fur, until his head cleared and he could figure out what to do next. Before he could ask, though, Jamie lifted his right hand and made it into a fist. He then straightened his fingers and crossed his thumb over his palm. He was repeating the shapes he'd made earlier. Next he made his hand into the shape of a crescent moon, and then he touched all his fingers to his thumb, except for his index finger, which he pointed straight up.

Jamie motioned for Ben to repeat all the shapes as he mouthed the corresponding letter.

Too tired to protest, Ben started copying the motions as Jamie continued: E. F. G. H. . . . Ben liked the feeling of the shapes on his hands, and he woke up a bit. Some letters were easy, like C and L and O and Z, because they looked just like the written letters, but others were harder to remember, like P and H and F.

They went through the alphabet a few times, then Jamie reached under a nearby shelf, pulled out a shoe box filled with Polaroids, and slid it toward Ben.

Ben understood that he wanted him to look at the photographs. He flipped through and saw images of dinosaur skeletons, dozens of views of the floating blue whale, and close-ups of bison, lizards, gorillas, mountain goats, elk, coyotes, and the wolves in their dioramas. Another section in the box had photos of museum visitors. There were endless studies of hairstyles, glasses, and clothes. One of the photos was the old woman they'd seen earlier at the wolf diorama.

"I told you she's here all the time! Once, I followed her and she walked up to the Keep Out sign on this room and ran her hand across it. I'd never noticed the door before. My dad works here so I stole a set of keys from the office and let myself in."

Jamie then showed Ben a picture of a woman with short blond hair and big gold glasses. He mouthed the words "My mom." She was standing next to a tree with a swing set nearby. *"She works late,"* Jamie wrote. *"I come home on the bus after school. I have my own house key. I spend the afternoons by myself. We live upstate."*

Ben didn't know what that meant, but it sounded far away. "You don't live in New York City?" he asked.

Jamie shook his head and flipped through the photos until he found a picture of a man wearing a crooked bow tie and a hat, walking toward the camera. He mouthed the words "My father." Instinctively, Ben touched the locket beneath his shirt.

"He lives here," Jamie wrote. *"I see him on holidays and weekends, and I live with him during the summer."*

Jamie reached into his pocket and pulled out the picture he'd taken of Ben. He slipped it into the box before pushing it back under the shelf.

Jamie pointed to Ben's suitcase and gestured for him to open it. Ben didn't want to, but Jamie's crooked smile convinced him it would be okay. Once he did, Jamie reached for the museum box. It was clear that he wanted to see what was inside. Ben hesitated again, but Jamie urged him to unlock the lock.

Everything was in its place: the two gray stones, his baby tooth, the little plastic game piece, the fossil, the bird skull, and the seashell turtle. Ben picked up each object and told Jamie a little bit about them. Unlike Billy, Jamie didn't tease him. He seemed to love hearing about them. He asked questions and put out his hand so he could touch all the items himself. Ben watched as Jamie held the objects, and for some reason, it made him happy. Only his mom had ever shown this much interest in his collection.

When they'd looked at everything, Jamie zipped up his green knapsack and slung it over his shoulder. He pointed to himself, then toward the door. *"It's getting late. I have to go. I'll be back tomorrow,"* he wrote. *"You sleep here. It's safe. Toilet's down the hall. Look out for the night watchman."* Jamie waved from the door and left.

Ben was exhausted and relieved to have a safe place to stay for the night. As he put the museum box back in his suitcase, he thought about Jamie taking such delicate care of the bird skull, and the seashell turtle, and the stromatolite.

He lay down on the fur and drew his knees up to his chest, but as soon as he closed his eyes, his thoughts turned to home. He was sure the people in the Duluth Children's Hospital had called his family when they found him missing. Were the police going to track him down here, to New York City? At least Robby was probably happy to have his room to himself for a while.

Ben imagined his mom sitting next to him, lifting his chin so he was looking up into her eyes. He waited for her to tell him what to do, to give him the perfect piece of advice. She had always liked him to figure things out for himself, though, and when he imagined her speaking, the only thing she said was, "We are all in the gutter, but some of us are looking at the stars." Then his mom disappeared, and he couldn't think of anything else to do, except to go back home.

Ben's head buzzed and his skin prickled. He turned on the flashlight and opened the locket. He stared into Daniel's face. Maybe he had been completely wrong from the start. Maybe this wasn't his father at all. Ben had been foolish to come all this way without more information. "Who are you?" he asked the picture. There was no answer. He wished he could stay long enough to find out why the wolves were here, but the guilt over worrying his family expanded in his chest, and he knew he had to return to Minnesota.

Ben was running through the snow again. The wind stung his face and he could barely breathe, but something felt different. There were no sounds of galloping footsteps, no howling, no crunching snow. Everything was silent, so he couldn't tell where the wolves were. Had they disappeared? Or were they right at his heels, about to pounce? Afraid to look back, he kept running until he woke up in a cold sweat, out of breath, with the caveman blanket wrapped around his legs.

Jamie didn't come back the next morning, and Ben didn't want to leave without thanking him and saying good-bye. Besides, he needed Jamie's help to call his aunt and uncle.

He was hungry, so he got up, changed his shirt, and headed into the museum, leaving the door unlocked. He used the bathroom, then went back to the café and finished the remains of another sandwich, a fruit cup, and some juice he found sitting on a deserted table. Then he made his way back to the wolf diorama and stared into the glass eyes of the running wolves.

Ben noticed a sign, mounted to the wall near the diorama, that he hadn't read yesterday.

Environment of the Wolf Group
Gunflint Lake, Minnesota

This typical December winter scene is placed at the margin of Gunflint Lake. Across the lake lies Ontario. Gunflint Lake forms part of the old fur-trading route extending westward from Lake Superior to Rainy Lake, which was originally selected to give the minimum number of portages.

The time is midnight. The temperature has fallen well below zero. The "curtain" type of northern lights blazes upward from the horizon. The constellations Ursa Major (the Big Dipper) and Ursa Minor (the Little Dipper) can be recognized.

Ben looked at the night sky painted on the curved wall at the back of the diorama. There it was . . . the Big Dipper. And in the tail of the Little Dipper, Ben could clearly see the North Star, but he'd never felt more lost in his life.

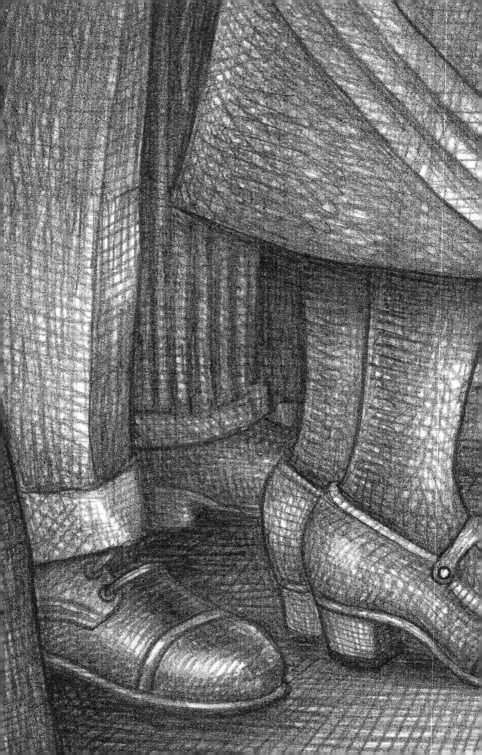

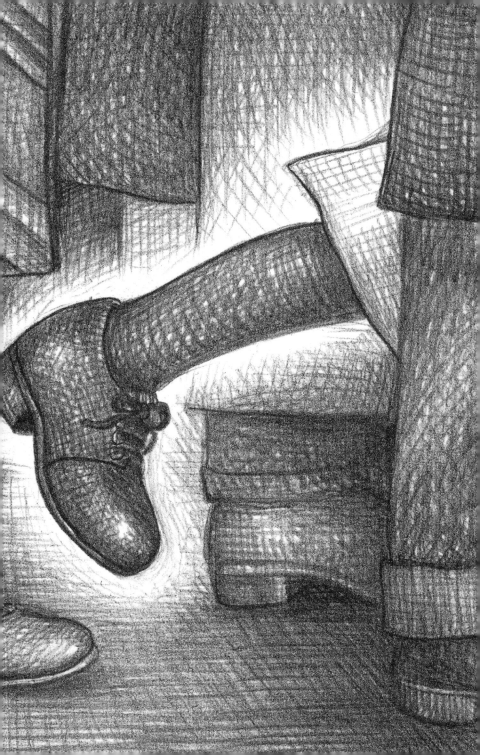

CABI

WON

HOW MUS

NETS

DERS

MS BEGAN

Ben had spent hours wandering around the museum. Then he'd returned to the secret room to wait for Jamie and unloaded his pockets, which he'd stuffed with things he'd found around the museum: a plastic dinosaur, a business card, a bobby pin, and a subway token.

He was rereading *Wonderstruck* when Jamie finally showed up that evening. He sat down next to Ben on the fur blanket and produced a couple of sandwiches and cans of soda from his green knapsack. Ben smiled, took one of the sandwiches, and drank some soda.

Jamie pulled out the notebook and wrote, *"Sorry it took me so long to get back. I forgot my dad was taking me on one of his work trips."*

Ben nodded. While he ate, Jamie reached under one of the shelves and slid out an old blue record player. It reminded Ben of his mom's. Jamie unsnapped the latch and opened the lid. He chose a record from a nearby stack and placed it on the turntable. As he was lowering the arm onto the record, he stopped and smacked his forehead. He made a face, indicating he'd done something stupid, then pointed to Ben and then to his own ears.

Ben said, "It's okay. You can listen. I'll feel the vibrations."

Jamie smiled and lowered the arm. Ben placed his hand over the fabric of the speaker built into the front of the record player and felt the music, just like his mom used to do. When the record ended, Ben said, "I have to go home, Jamie. Can you tell your dad about me and ask him to call my family?"

The strangest look crossed Jamie's face. *"Okay,"* he wrote. *"But first I have a surprise for you! My dad is working late tonight so I have a few hours. Follow me."*

When Ben didn't move, Jamie wrote, *"I promise I'll talk to my dad later."*

The museum had closed for the night and it was eerily still. Jamie led Ben down long hallways and through many doors, some of which he had to unlock with his set of keys. Most of the lights had been turned off, plunging everything into darkness. The beam of Jamie's flashlight lit the floor ahead of them. When they came upon a night watchman sitting and reading a book at the end of a corridor, Jamie pulled Ben around the corner and down another hallway.

He opened a door marked ELECTRICS. Carefully, he led Ben through another door to a row of folding seats and pushed gently on his shoulders, indicating he should sit. When Ben's eyes adjusted to the darkness, he made out the dim glow from a control panel where Jamie stood. A giant object, like a mechanical insect, appeared in the center of the room. It turned and spun and suddenly the ceiling lit up with stars.

Ben gasped. The planetarium!

Jamie came and sat next to him as the sky filled with shooting stars. The projector rotated, the view changed, and the boys found themselves *inside* a meteor, hurtling across the sky. They flew to the moon and bounced between craters. One by one, the planets drifted into view, and soon they were out beyond the solar system, gazing down on the universe like ancient gods. Ben thought of the glow-in-the-dark stars in his room, and the Big Dipper, and the quote about the stars, and his mom. The glowing lights above him spun and swirled, tracing endless patterns against the perfect dome of the ceiling like a million electric fireflies making constellations in the dark.

When the show ended and they had been brought gently back to Earth, Jamie led Ben out into the museum again. They passed the shadow-covered elephants and the hanging black birds that kept watch over the museum. Ben pointed up as they paused beneath the gray silhouette of the giant whale. Around them, all the dioramas were sunk in darkness. The glass turned to mirrors in the dim light, so the boys saw their reflections as they passed. They waved their arms and made faces in the mirrors. Behind their reflections, from certain angles, the animals peered out like ghosts from the Serengeti. For a moment, Ben found it hard to imagine the museum was ever full of light and bustling with people. The building felt permanently haunted.

Jamie, smiling broadly, turned on the flashlight and ushered Ben into a rickety old elevator. He slid the metal gate shut and pushed down on a long bronze handle. The elevator jerked and lowered slowly into the basement, where Jamie led Ben down another maze of hallways to large double doors peeling with a century's worth of paint. A sign on the door read WORKSHOP in stenciled black letters. Below that, someone had handwritten *Abandon all hope ye who enter here!*

Inside, Jamie wandered from table to table, picking up metal tools and jars of mysterious liquids that glowed like amber. Ben stared in awe, trying to imagine what each one was for.

After a few minutes, Jamie mouthed the word "more!" and took Ben to a series of vast storage rooms. Ben looked around in amazement. He ran his hands across dusty old dinosaur bones, rows of little birds on wooden perches, seashells, fossils, bugs, ancient clothing, spearheads, turquoise jewelry, ivory buttons, and a thousand other fascinating things.

The boys explored for a while, and then Jamie led them down a long hallway filled on one side with black metal filing cabinets stacked five drawers high for as far as the eye could see. Teetering on top of the filing cabinets were piles of discarded furniture, including an old empty card catalog, even bigger than the one in his mom's library.

Ben stared down the row of filing cabinets. There had to be thousands of drawers here! He opened one and looked inside. Long hanging files with little tabs extended to the back of the drawer. Ben pulled out a piece of paper, a detailed receipt for the acquisition of a golden cup in 1913. He read it quickly, and then removed an old photo of the museum. Ben noticed right away that the entrance was different. He was wondering how else the museum had changed over the years, when Jamie motioned him back into the main hallway of the museum.

In the darkness, they retraced their path until Ben found himself in front of the dark mirror of the wolf diorama. The electric moonlight had been turned off, and when Jamie shined the flashlight inside, four glittering glass eyes flashed back.

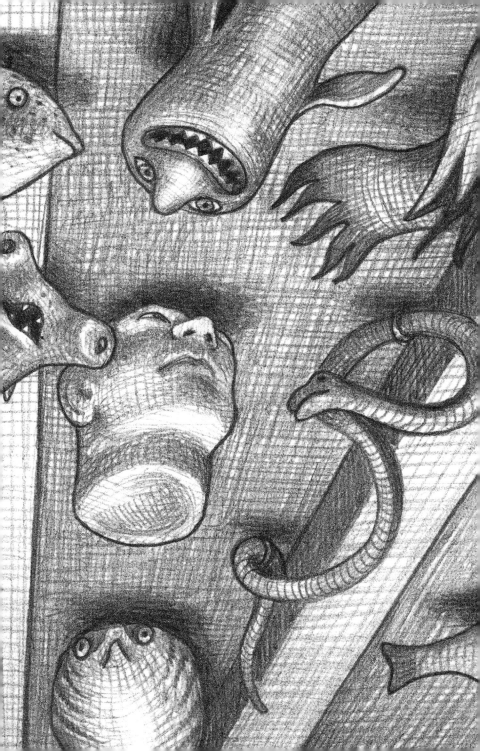

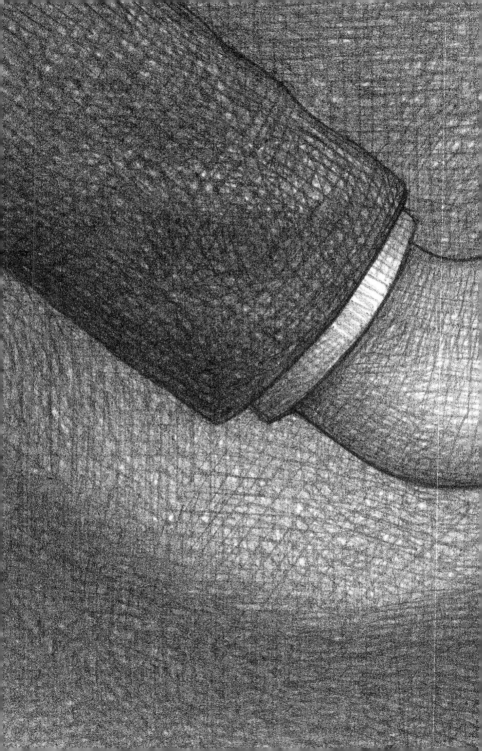

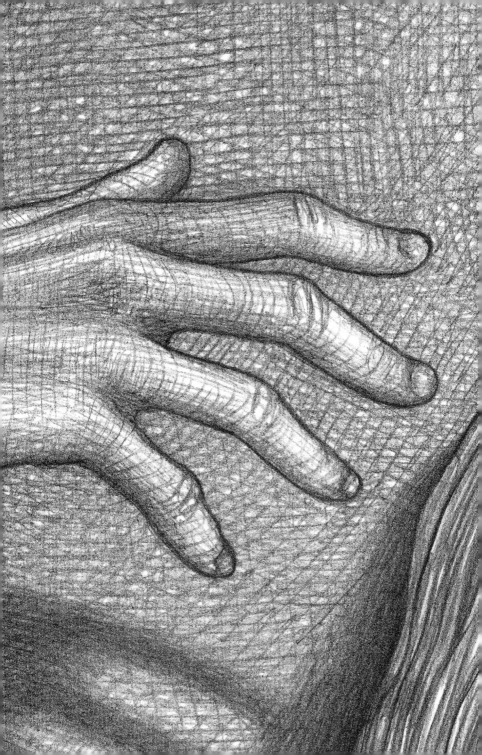

When they had finally made it back to the secret room, the two boys sat on the caveman fur and caught their breath.

"That was amazing!" Ben said, shaking his head. "Thank you!"

Jamie's face glowed. He took another picture of Ben and handed Ben the camera. Ben took a picture of Jamie and they laid the images next to each other on the blanket to develop. Jamie passed Ben the flashlight as he wrote a long note in the notebook, his tongue sticking out between his teeth.

"I've never shown anyone the museum before. Your wolf box made me think you'd like it." Jamie paused for a moment and looked quickly at Ben. In that split second, Ben saw something in Jamie's glance, something that connected the two of them, beyond the secret room and a love for the museum.

In a moment, the pen was moving again. *"I don't have any friends here. No one likes the things I like. No one shares this stuff with me. Not even my dad, who's been working in the planetarium for two years, really knows, or cares, about what I do all day. Only you."*

Ben looked at the words *only you,* and he wanted to tell Jamie he felt the same way, but he let Jamie keep writing.

"I wish my dad really cared about me."

"I'm sure he does," Ben said. "Maybe he's just busy."

Jamie shrugged and mouthed the word "maybe."

"Talk to him," Ben said, trying to imagine what it would be like to talk to his own dad.

Instead of answering, Jamie started doodling in the notebook, drawing long dotted lines and arrows. Ben traced his finger along the lines and Jamie laughed. *"Sorry! Sometimes when I'm thinking or when I'm bored, I make up games for myself. I like to draw maps."*

When he read this, Ben said, "I know! And you follow people around the museum, too!"

Jamie smiled. *"I like having a place that's my own, to organize my photographs and listen to music."*

Ben nodded. "My mom and I liked listening to music together while we were reading. She was a librarian."

"Was? What does she do now?"

Ben tried to speak, but the words wouldn't come. He took the notebook and the pen and wrote about his mom and the car accident and living at his cousins' house.

"Oh," Jamie mouthed, when he finished reading what Ben had written. "I'm sorry."

Ben didn't answer.

"Where's your dad?" Jamie wrote.

Ben shrugged.

"Are your parents divorced, too?"

Ben shook his head. When he offered no further explanations, Jamie wrote, *"Are there really wolves in Gunflint Lake?"*

Ben nodded.

"So, why did you do it?"

"Do what?" Ben said.

Jamie pointed to Ben's suitcase and mimed running away with his fingers. *"It's far, isn't it?"*

Ben looked down for a moment and took a deep breath. "After the lightning hit me, I was in the hospital in Duluth for a long time. I could see the bus station from my window." Ben paused and Jamie nodded, as if encouraging him to go on.

"My cousin Janet owed me a favor. When she came to visit, I asked if she could bring me a book I liked and a necklace of my mom's. I also asked for clean clothes, my museum box, and money from my mom's rainy-day fund so I could buy some food in the vending machines. On her next visit, she brought everything in a suitcase."

"Did she know you were going to"—and Jamie made his fingers run again.

"I don't think so. She wouldn't have brought all the stuff if she did. That night I changed into my own clothes, snuck out of the hospital, and went to the bus station. I was halfway to New York before I realized I should have left a note for my family."

"But you still haven't said why you"— and Jamie made the running motion with his fingers.

Ben paused for a minute, then said, "I wanted to find my father."

"He lives in New York?"

"I thought he did."

Ben could tell from Jamie's expression that he needed to explain more.

"I've never met my dad. My mom never talked about him. When I was in the hospital, I asked my aunt if she knew anything, but she said she didn't. I had found my dad's address in my mom's things after she died. I thought she might have been planning this trip for me, and I felt like I had to come. It's strange, thinking about it now. It was almost as if . . . something came over me. . . . One minute I had the idea to find my father, and the next minute I was on a bus to New York."

Ben shook his head, still in shock that he'd actually done it. "As soon as I arrived, I went to his apartment, but he doesn't live there anymore. I had one other clue, a bookmark from Kincaid's that he wrote on. I thought they might remember him. That's why I was there the day we met."

"I tried to tell you Kincaid's isn't"—Jamie stopped

writing and held the pen in midair.

Ben looked from Jamie to the pen, then to the paper, unsure why Jamie was pausing. At last, the pen connected with the paper again and he finished the sentence.

—*"isn't open anymore."*

"I could see that!"

"I didn't know you were deaf then," Jamie wrote.

The two boys sat for a while, looking around the secret room. It was as if they were both waiting for something to happen, but neither knew what it was.

"I wish I could stay here longer. But my aunt is probably worried sick. I have to go back to Gunflint Lake."

Jamie shook his head. *"First you have to practice signing."*

Ben smiled as he made an "Okay" sign.

Jamie showed Ben the letters again, and they spelled each other's names. They practiced spelling different words and after a while Ben was able to sign most of the alphabet.

Jamie paused and picked up the notebook. *"My mom's*

coming to visit tomorrow, so I'll be away."

"I have to go home, Jamie. You said you'd ask your dad to help me."

Jamie looked at Ben as if he was trying to figure out something. He finally wrote: *"I'm worried my dad will get mad at me."*

"Why? You helped me. Isn't that a good thing?""

Jamie reached into his pocket and gave Ben his set of keys. *"Stay and explore a little longer and we'll figure out what to do. Just be careful. Leave the door open for me. I'll see you in two days!"*

Ben wrote down a number on a page in the notebook, which he handed back to Jamie. "Will *you* call my aunt and uncle for me, then? Tell them I'm okay, and they can come get me at the museum."

Jamie ripped out the piece of paper and said, "Sure." He reached into his bag and pulled out some sandwiches and apples for Ben. Then he pressed the notebook and pen into Ben's hand. "For you."

"Thanks. Please don't forget to call."

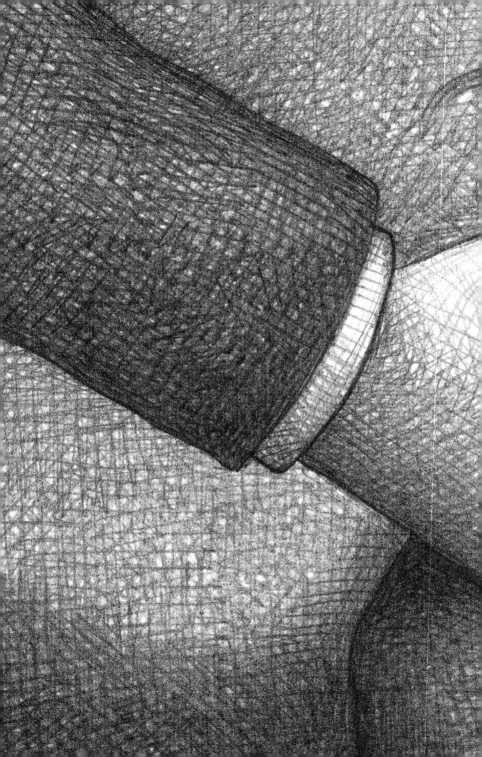

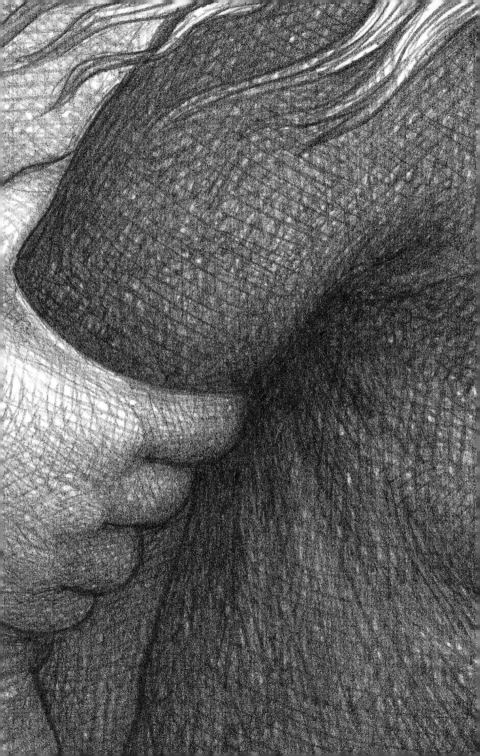

The next morning, Ben headed to the wolf diorama. He read the sign on the wall over and over again, trying to make sense of how his dream got here, behind glass in the museum. He stared at the North Star. He wished that he was with his mom in her library, where everything was safe and numbered and organized by the Dewey decimal system. Ben wished the *world* was organized by the Dewey decimal system. That way you'd be able to find whatever you were looking for, like the meaning of your dream, or your dad.

If only the card catalog in the hall of filing cabinets wasn't empty. Ben might have been able to look up information about the diorama.

Then he remembered the receipt for the golden cup he'd found inside the filing cabinets. What else might be filed away in there?

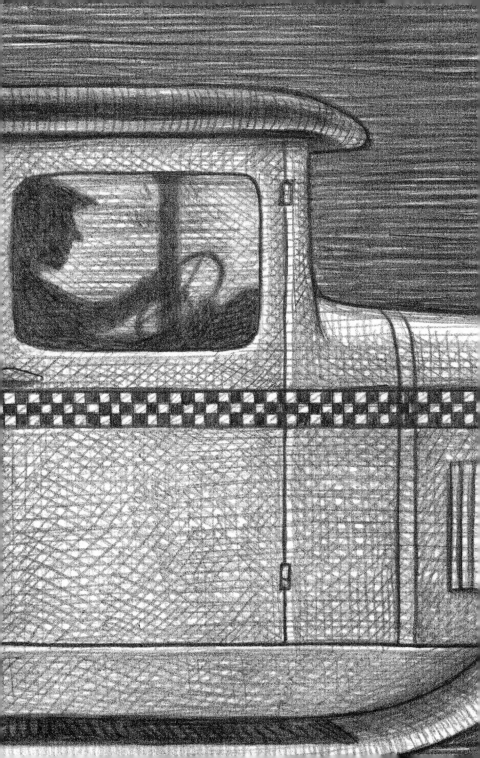

Maxwell House Coffee
Good to the last drop

CHEVROLET

RESCUE BRAND DENTAL CREAM

TIRES
CAPIT

BROTHERS TONIC

CANDY

The files stretched from one end of the huge hall to the other. Each drawer had a silver handle and a little framed card indicating what was inside. Ben ran the length of the hallway until he came to the section of files for the letter D. He counted and was amazed that there were fifty-eight different drawers all labeled *Dioramas*.

One by one, he opened them and found hanging files stuffed with papers and photographs, legal pads, and notes. There seemed to be files for every single diorama in the entire museum but nothing labeled *Gunflint Lake*. There were no files for *Wolves*, either. He tried *Minnesota* and *Night* before figuring out they were organized by halls. He found a little tab with the words *Hall of North American Mammals* typed on a small white card. He flipped past files labeled *ALASKA BROWN BEAR, Canoe Bay, Alaska Peninsula; JAGUAR, Box Canyon, Near Guaymos, Western Sonora, Mexico;* and *WAPITI, Trappers Lake Basin, Horseshoe Range, Colorado.* Finally he came to *WOLF, Gunflint Lake, Minnesota.* There were four files with that title! Ben took a deep breath and opened them.

In the first file, he saw beautiful photographs of birds, animals, and trees that he knew well, like black-billed cuckoos, gulls, raccoons, otters, aspen, white spruce, and birch. Most were black-and-white but a few were in color. There were photos of the arching sky, and the Gunflint stones, and wide expanses of snow. Some pictures were out of focus, and a few had arrows and circles drawn on them with a pen. On the bottom of most of the photos it said *1965*.

In the second file, Ben found drawings of Gunflint Lake. There were pictures of trees and the lake he'd left behind and every square inch of the property all around his house, as well as the sky at day and night and the phases of the moon. The drawings were done in pencil or charcoal, and the lines were swift and bold. Ben saw a sketch that he recognized immediately as the cabin on his family's property, and he shivered.

The third file was filled with hundreds of sketches of wolves in every possible position. Ben marveled at the way they ran and sat and jumped across the pages. Their eyes were bright with intelligence, and he could almost feel the muscles beneath their fur.

The fourth file contained legal papers, contracts, letters, receipts, charts, and tickets. A little slip of paper, folded in half, was wedged in the bottom of the file. He unfolded it and saw that it was a receipt. The purple ink was fading, but he could read the date, *1969*. On the back was a handwritten note in black ink:

Dinner tomorrow. Meet at Kincaid's. 8 pm. Love, M.

Kincaid's? M? Ben felt a faint ripple of electricity rush across the surface of his skin. Was this the same Kincaid's he'd been looking for? And was it the same M who'd written a note inside *Wonderstruck?*

A shadow stretching across the files at the end of the hallway caught Ben's attention. Someone was coming! Ben panicked and grabbed the files. Stealing them was easier than he would have guessed. No one tried to stop him as he moved through the museum, holding the precious papers.

Once he was safely inside the secret room, he closed the door, placed the files on the floor, and collapsed onto the fur. He laid aside the first three files and opened the fourth one.

Carefully, he slipped the receipt with the note about Kincaid's into his pocket.

Ben continued to thumb through the rest of the file, past meaningless papers and ledgers, until a carbon copy of a letter caught his eye. It was on official-looking stationery from the museum.

May 12, 1964

Dear Miss Wilson,

I am writing to you as an employee of the American Museum of Natural History, in New York City. I have recently agreed to undertake an exciting assignment to create a new diorama based on the flora and fauna of the Gunflint Lake region of Minnesota. My colleagues and I plan to arrive in Minneapolis sometime in October, and then we will travel by car up to the lake region, which I understand is about a five-hour trip. Since you are the town librarian, I am reaching out to you, hoping you might be able to help us as we research all the elements needed for the creation of our diorama. We plan to spend about two months in Gunflint Lake, to give us adequate time to understand the land and the animals. It's our sincere wish to work with you. I will be sketching and taking extensive photographs during the course of the entire trip. At the moment, we are also looking for places we can stay. Any suggestions you might have would be greatly appreciated. You can contact me at the address above.

Thank you very much,

Daniel Lobel, Exhibition Preparator

The American Museum of Natural History

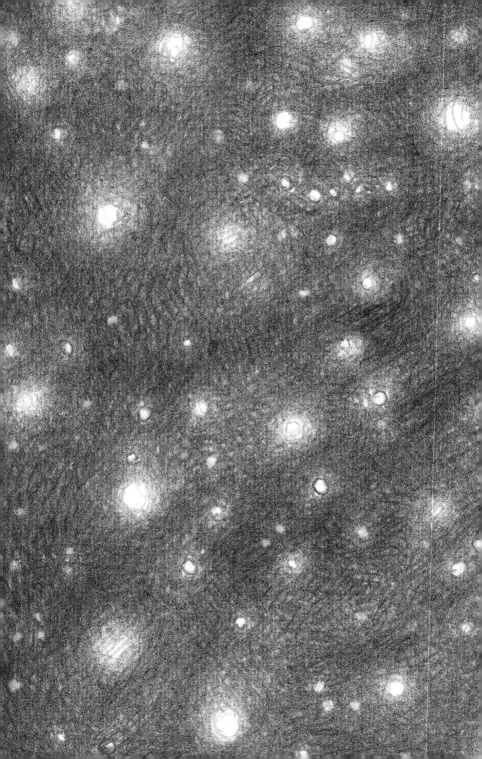

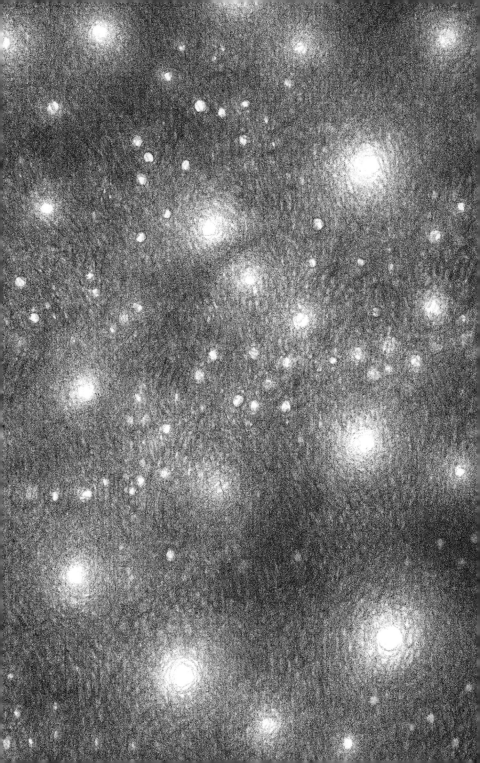

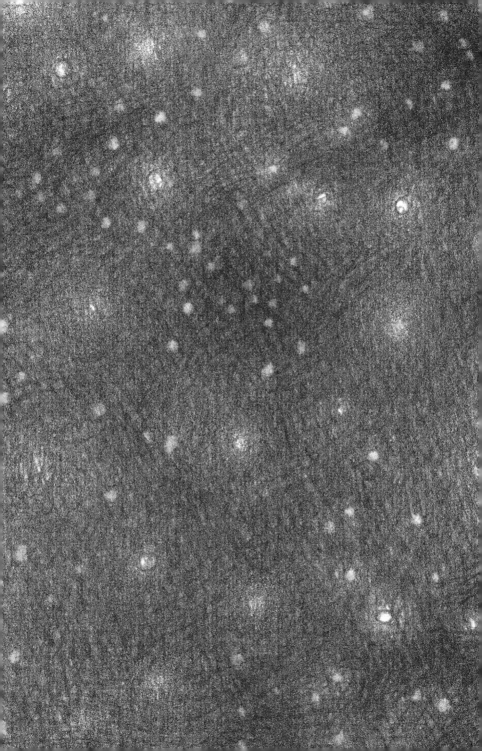

Ben rushed through the museum until he arrived at the information desk in the entrance hall. He was sure his heart was going to come crashing through his chest. He ran to the front of the line and said breathlessly, "I'm looking for Daniel Lobel. He works here!"

The woman started speaking, but Ben interrupted her. "I need to find him right now. He's my dad!"

The woman's lips moved again.

Ben thought she was asking him if he was lost. "Please just look him up!"

The woman seemed worried. She glanced back at the long line of people waiting to ask her a question, then put on her glasses and pulled out a black book from one of the drawers in her desk. Stamped in white on the cover of the book were the words *Museum Directory, 1976–1977*. She flipped through the pages, brought the book closer to her face, and frowned. She then turned to Ben. Her mouth moved as she shook her head.

"He's got to be there! Look him up again, please!"

The woman put her finger to her lips and he knew he must have been speaking too loudly.

She ran her finger down one of the pages, then turned the book toward Ben, showing him the names *Lisky, Katherine* and *Logan, Michael.* She tapped the names, indicating that his father's name would have been between them if he worked at the museum.

Ben felt his whole body sag.

The woman closed the book, picked up the phone, smiled in a strained way, and said something. Ben watched as she spoke into the phone, hung up, and raised one hand, indicating he should wait. Had she called someone who knew Daniel? Ben hopped from foot to foot, impatiently waiting as the woman turned to help other people in the line. He watched the minutes tick by on a clock behind her desk. At last she nodded toward someone on the other side of the room. Ben spun around.

To his horror, a guard was heading toward them. The woman must have called security. Ben ran into the crowd and disappeared back into the museum. His heart raced. His thoughts spun.

Even if his dad didn't work at the museum anymore, surely *someone* here must remember him.

Using Jamie's keys, he made his way back down to the workroom where he and Jamie had explored the night before. He pushed open the door that said *Abandon all hope ye who enter here!* Inside, two young men were hunched over their desks. A young woman in the corner poured some kind of liquid into a mold. All three of them looked up when Ben entered the room.

"I'm looking for Daniel Lobel," he said. "He used to

work here. He made the wolf diorama!'"

The three workers looked at one another and shook their heads. Two of them started to speak at the same time. Ben tried to figure out what they were saying. One of the men got up and walked toward Ben. He couldn't read his lips, but he was sure he knew what he was saying. None of them knew his father.

Before they could call security, Ben darted out of the room and ran as fast as he could. Soon he found himself back at the wolf diorama. Out of breath, he knelt down and stared into the wolves' eyes. They seemed to burn with secrets Ben was sure he'd never know. He put his hand up against the sheet of glass that separated him from the running wolves. He pictured them leaping toward him through the glass and swallowing him whole.

Ben didn't know how long he stayed there before he finally returned to the secret room. The files lay scattered across the floor. He read through them again and noticed that all the correspondences relating to his father stopped in 1969, and he figured that must have been when he left the museum.

Ben ran his hands along the cluttered shelves, searching for a good place to store the papers. For the first time, he noticed how fancy the shelves were, with all sorts of curly shapes and elaborate designs carved into the supports. Why would anyone decorate a storage room?

All at once, Ben remembered the checkerboard pattern on the floor. He moved aside the caveman fur, grabbed an old piece of cloth, and rubbed away the dirt. More of the pattern appeared. It looked as if it had been painted to look like marble. Ben studied it and gazed again at the fancy shelves. The whole room started to feel oddly familiar.

Ben had been in this room for a few days now, but he realized he hadn't really been *looking* at it. Behind the furniture piled in the corner of the room was a rectangular object about a foot taller than he was. It was covered in a tattered old piece of fabric with huge water stains. Ben walked over and moved the furniture aside. As he pulled off the cloth, a cloud of dust rose up, and he coughed.

Beneath the fabric was an old wood cabinet. The front was filled with little drawers and doors, each with a small picture on it. A few broken seashells and pieces of coral were attached to the top of the cabinet. Ben couldn't stop staring at it. His skin started buzzing again as he realized what he was looking at.

The shelves, the floor, the cabinet . . . they were all exactly the same as the illustration he'd seen in *Wonderstruck.*

He was standing inside his father's book!

Thank
Walt

fig. 26

Ben grabbed his copy of *Wonderstruck* and opened it to the illustration of the room. He looked from the picture to the cabinet, and found himself staring at the broken seashells on top of the old piece of furniture. The colors and the shapes reminded him of something, and he moved closer to inspect them. The illustration showed that this crown of shells and coral had once stood very tall, with all sorts of ornate decorations at the base that were drawn too small to see clearly. There was very little left of the crown now. The dried cement still had a few shells stuck to it, though, and the indentations of other shells, long lost, could be seen, like tiny fossils.

Ben's gaze rested on one of the indentations. Slowly, as if underwater, he tucked *Wonderstruck* into his back pocket, picked up his museum box, and opened it. He took out the seashell turtle and found the indentation on the cabinet again. Just as he had suspected, the turtle fit perfectly, like the last piece in a mysterious puzzle he didn't quite understand. How could this be? How could a tiny seashell turtle that was part of a museum exhibition in New York City decades ago make its way halfway across the country to his house in Minnesota?

Ben tried to put it all together. Did the turtle once belong to his dad? Had he given it to his mom? Is that why she had given it to Ben? What had his dad been doing in this room? And why had his mom kept so many secrets?

The files Ben had stolen caught his eye, and he looked around for a place to store them. He opened the cabinet. It was empty. Carefully, he placed the papers inside, then lay down on the fur blanket.

He only meant to rest for a moment, but before long, Ben was running desperately through the snow again. Someone grabbed his foot and Ben yelled, "Stop, Robby!" He sat bolt upright and opened his eyes. It must have already been morning because there in front of him was Jamie, carrying his green knapsack. What time was it? Ben shot a quick glance at the cabinet of wonders. Sitting on top was Ben's seashell turtle.

As soon as he was able to think more clearly, Ben asked, "Did you call my aunt and uncle?"

Jamie's eyes went wide, like a deer caught in the headlights of an oncoming car. He mouthed the words "I forgot."

Relieved, Ben said, "It's okay. I'm not ready to leave." He was still dazed from everything he'd learned. He started telling Jamie about the wolf diorama, and his dad, and how no one he'd talked to remembered him. Ben got more excited as he spoke, recounting each revelation and each disappointment.

Jamie just looked down and nodded absently.

"Maybe your dad knows someone who remembers . . . "

Jamie picked up the notebook and pen. *"He's working."*

Ben must have looked disappointed, because Jamie gave him a big smile, as if to cheer him up. *"I have a present for you."*

He reached into his knapsack and pulled out a large yellow book. The cover read *Dictionary of American Sign Language, edited by Noah Fabricant and Lydia Del Ono, illustrated with over 250 drawings and indexed for easy cross-referencing. Learn sign language NOW!*

To be polite, Ben opened it. He stared at the tiny pen-and-ink drawings of hands and arms with arrows pointing up, down, forward, and back. It looked like a book of codes. How would Ben ever learn them all?

Anxiously, he flipped through the book. Midway through he found a bookmark tucked between the pages. To his surprise Jamie tried to grab it away. Thinking he was playing some kind of game, Ben snatched it back.

Across the top it read *Kincaid Books.*

It looked just like the other bookmark Ben had found: It had the same striped awning, the same books, the same cat . . . only the address was different.

Ben looked at Jamie, confused. "Is there another Kincaid's?"

Jamie didn't answer.

Ben stared at the bookmark.

"Jamie, the bookstore still exists?"

Jamie had the most incomprehensible expression on his face. Why was he acting so strange? Why wouldn't he look at Ben? And then it dawned on him. "The other night I told you I was looking for Kincaid's. You told me it was closed."

Jamie said nothing.

"Why didn't you tell me it had just moved?"

Finally, Jamie wrote, *"I didn't know. I just found out yester"*—

"You're lying to me."

"I'm not."

"Tell me the truth," Ben said.

Jamie's hand shook as he wrote, *"It's stupid."*

Ben pointed to the notebook, silently commanding Jamie to write more.

"I was afraid if you found your father, he'd take you away and you wouldn't come anymore. And if you didn't find him, you'd go back to Gunflint Lake and I'd never see you again."

"But . . . what did you think I was going to do? I can't live here forever."

Ben saw Jamie mouth the words "I know, I know." Then Jamie wrote, *"I just wanted you to stay and be my friend."* He rubbed his eyes, then stared at the floor.

Was Ben supposed to comfort Jamie, to tell him it was okay that he betrayed him? Didn't Jamie know that he wanted to be friends, too? But wouldn't a true friend help him find his father?

Jamie looked up, blinked a few times, and then wrote again. His face changed and now he seemed quite determined, pressing the pen hard into the paper.

"And, just so you know, I DID try to tell you the book-store was still open. The first day I met you. I pointed in the direction of the new store, but you didn't listen and you ran away. How was I supposed to know you were deaf?"

Ben just stared at the words, as if he could no longer understand their meaning. It felt like a hole had opened up in the floor and he'd slipped through.

In a daze, he took the notebook and pen, stood up, and walked to the cabinet. He grabbed the seashell turtle from its perch and stuffed it into his pocket, along with the new bookmark.

Then, without looking back, he headed for the door.

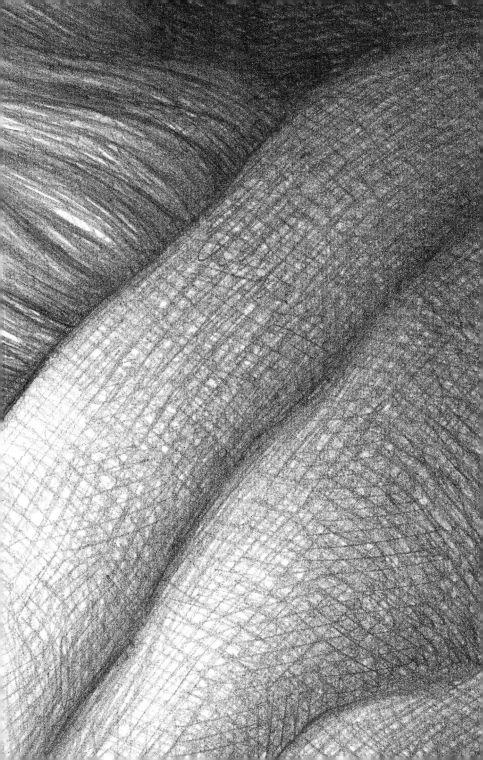

PART THREE

Ben hadn't been outside in days. The city was still burning hot, and he was sweating by the time he reached Kincaid's.

The store was larger than he expected. Books spilled off shelves, covered tables, and teetered in piles. Sunshine poured in through the front windows, lighting up the dust as it spiraled through the air. The air inside was cool and smelled like old paper. There was also the faint aroma of bread from the bakery next door. In the center of the store, a staircase rose to an overstuffed balcony. Every step was lined with more books. There were no customers, and no one behind the counter. The only sign of life was a sleeping black cat near the cash register. A battered clock hanging at an angle behind the counter said 4:15.

Ben wiped his forehead with the inside of his shirt, then walked to the counter.

"Hello? Hello?" He hoped he was speaking loudly. When no one emerged, he knocked on the counter. Still, no one answered. Only the cat responded, jumping to the floor and bolting up the stairs.

Ben decided to follow the cat. Maybe the owner was upstairs. He climbed the steps. There didn't seem to be anyone around. He was thirsty and couldn't remember the last time he'd eaten. A wave of nausea passed through him and for a moment he thought he might be sick right there on the stairs. He sat on a step and put his head between his knees. He thought about Jamie, and took out his notebook. He flipped through the pages, looking at the things Jamie had written.

"I just wanted you to stay and be my friend."

An icy blast from the air conditioner made Ben shiver. Slowly, he lifted his head, unsure how long he should sit on the steps, waiting for someone to appear.

Ben recognized the old woman as soon as she stepped through the door. She was the one who had stopped in front of the wolf diorama that first day with Jamie.

She wiped her face with a handkerchief as she walked up to an old man with round black glasses who had appeared behind the counter. She kissed him on the cheek. They didn't speak to each other, but their hands began to move, making all sorts of shapes and patterns. It took only a moment for Ben to figure out that they were using sign language!

After a few exchanges, the old man turned his head toward the phone, held up one hand to the old woman, and then picked up the receiver. The old woman continued to sign with the old man while he spoke on the phone. Ben marveled at how the man could have two conversations at once. He figured that only the woman was deaf, since the man was using the phone. The couple kept signing after the old man hung up. At several points, he and the old woman laughed. Ben was amazed by the speed of their hands and the pleasure in their faces. He didn't think he'd ever be able to sign that quickly, no matter how much he studied. He thought about the alphabet Jamie had taught him, but his mind went blank when he tried to remember the letters.

Holding the notebook and pen in one hand, Ben

started to stand. But his left leg had fallen asleep beneath him, and before he could brace himself, it buckled and he toppled down the stairs. He landed on the floor with a hard thud amid an avalanche of books.

Ben looked up into the terrified eyes of the old man and old woman. He groaned as they helped him sit up. The old man was speaking to him. Ben shook his head and pointed to his ears. "I can't hear." When they began to sign, Ben shook his head again. "I don't know sign language." Slowly, he looked around until he spotted the notebook and pen, which had fallen nearby.

The old man retrieved them and wrote: *"Anything broken?"*

Ben stretched his arms and legs and said, "I don't think so." But he was rattled from the fall. "May I have some water?"

The old man nodded and disappeared into the back. Ben noticed that the old woman had become very still. She was studying him with the oddest expression. It looked like confusion and wonder and sadness, all at the same time.

The old man returned with the water. As Ben drank it, he watched the old woman sign to the old man and then look back at Ben. She reached forward and touched the locket around Ben's neck. He glanced down and saw that it had opened.

The old woman covered her mouth with her hand and then grabbed on to the old man. Tears spilled down her cheeks. She wiped her eyes with her handkerchief and then placed her hand on the side of Ben's face. Her thumb brushed momentarily across his skin.

A thousand questions ran through his mind, but

before he could ask any of them, the old woman reached for the pen and notebook.

Ben watched her trembling hand as it held the pen over the paper before she began to write. She then turned the pad so he could read what she had written.

"Ben?"

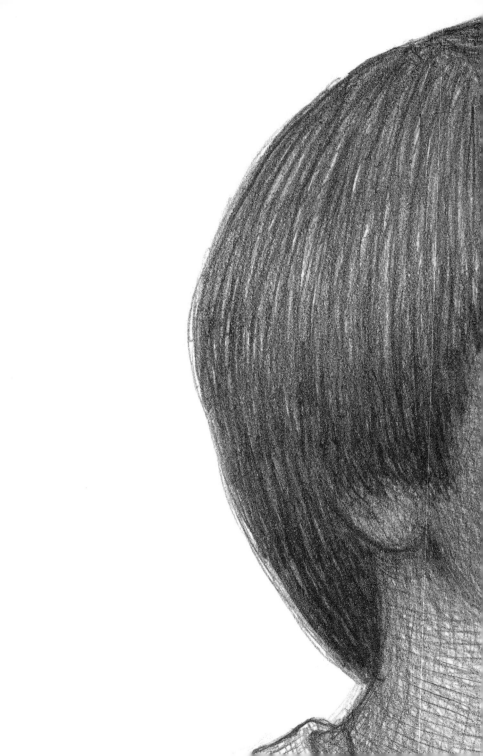

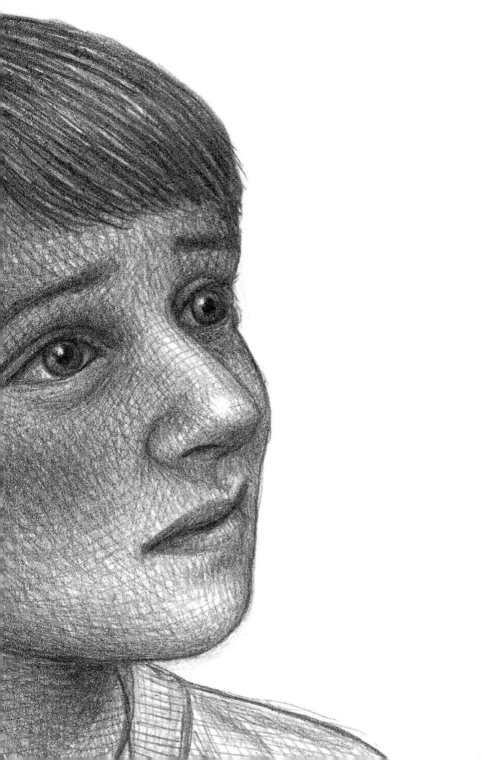

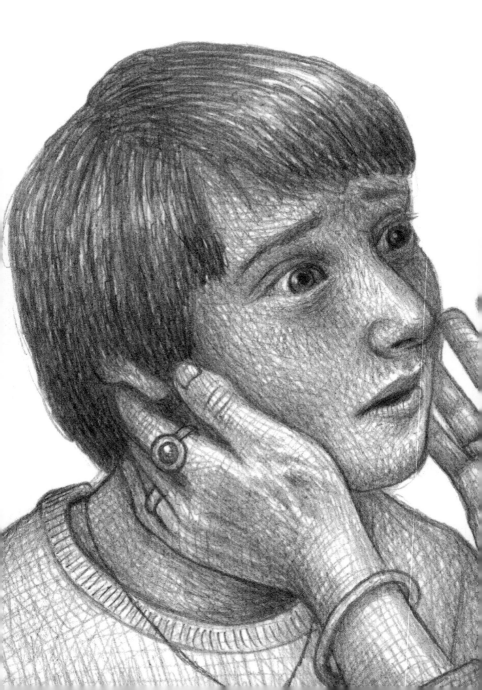

The old woman's hands were warm. She pulled Ben to her and held him tightly. What was going on? Ben pulled back and said, "How do you know my name?"

The old woman seemed to be able to read his lips, but the old man also translated Ben's words into signs. The woman took the pen, pointed to herself, and wrote, *"Rose."* She pointed the pen toward the old man. *"My brother, Walter."*

Ben asked again, "How do you know my name? Do you know my father?"

Walter signed Ben's questions, and Rose wrote in the notebook, *"Where is your mother?"*

Ben didn't know how to answer. It would take so long to explain.

Then he remembered the pages he'd written for Jamie. He flipped back in the notebook and handed it to Rose. He rubbed the locket between his fingers and waited while she and Walter read his story.

When they were done, Rose hugged Ben again. He resisted at first, but finally he let himself be held, and it was comforting, even from a stranger.

Rose pulled back and wiped her eyes. *"I'm so sorry about your mom,"* she wrote. *"Do your aunt and uncle know where you are?"*

Ben shook his head.

"They must be so worried! Write down their phone number." She gestured toward her brother and held her hand to her ear like a phone, indicating Walter would make the call.

Ben wrote down the number, relieved that his aunt and uncle would finally know where he was and that he was safe.

"How did you find us?" Rose wrote.

Ben's pockets were full of stuff, but he rooted around until he found the original bookmark and the new one from the dictionary Jamie had brought him. He unfolded them and handed them both to Rose. She and Walter read Danny's note to Elaine on the back of the first one. Then Ben reached into his back pocket and pulled out one more thing.

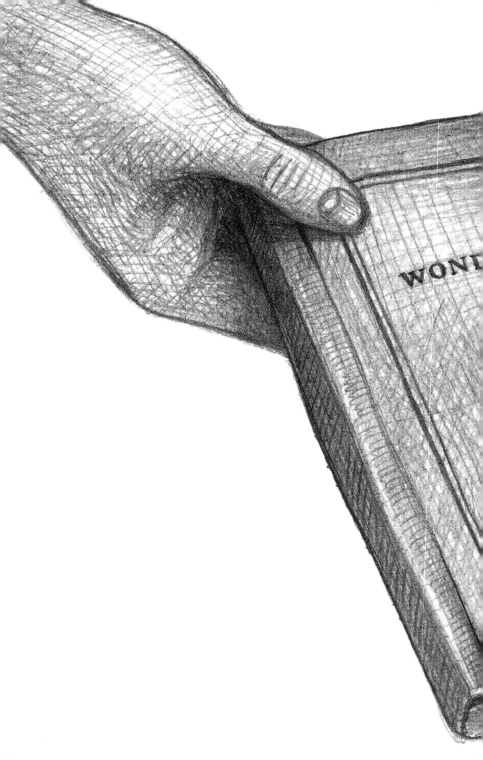

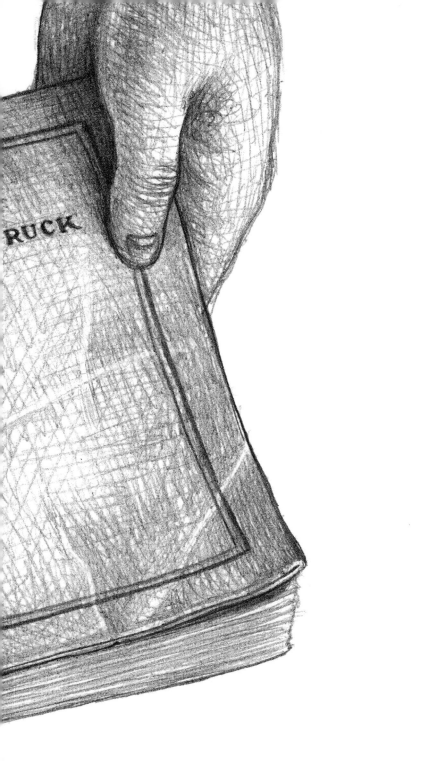

As the old woman touched the book, Ben said again, "Please tell me how you know my name."

Reading his lips, Rose wrote, *"We met a long time ago."*

Except for the time in the museum a few days earlier, Ben was sure he'd never seen this woman before.

"How did we meet?" Ben asked as Walter translated. "When?"

"It's a long story, but it starts here. . . ." Rose pointed to the red M opposite the title page of *Wonderstruck.* *"Walter worked at the museum before he opened this store. He gave this book to me when I was young. I drew the roses and leaves. Like a signature."*

"I don't understand. It's signed M and you said your name is Rose."

Rose turned to Walter, who translated the words she missed.

"M is for Mother," she wrote.

"You are Danny's mother?" As Ben said the words, it dawned on him what this meant.

Rose's face somehow changed before his eyes. Her skin, her white hair, and her slender fingers no longer belonged to a stranger. He wrote, *"You're my grandmother."*

Rose wiped the tears from her eyes and smiled.

Ben hugged her again. He felt the soft fabric of her

blouse, and her ribs moving as she breathed. After a few moments, he pulled away and asked, "Where is he? I came all the way from Minnesota to find him."

Walter translated, but the old woman seemed lost in thought. *"What do you know about him?"* she finally wrote.

Ben spoke in a rush, but Walter kept up with him. "I don't know anything about him. My mom never talked about him. After she died, I found *Wonderstruck* and the note on the bookmark. That's how I learned his name was Daniel and that he lived in New York." Ben explained about going to his apartment and ending up at the museum and finding the wolf diorama and the files. "I read a letter he wrote to my mom, so I know that he used to work in the museum, and that he made the diorama, and that they must have met when he came to Minnesota to do research. But that's all I know!"

When Walter finished signing for Rose, she signed back. Then she nodded and wrote, *"I will answer all your questions, Ben, as best I can, but first, tell me if you've eaten."*

Ben shook his head. He had almost forgotten how hungry he was. Walter went into the back and returned with a sandwich and a cup of orange juice, as well as a plate full of pretzels, which Ben ate quickly.

After Walter had taken the dishes back to the office, he

and Rose signed something and then she wrote, *"I want to answer your questions, but I can't do it here. We have to take a subway ride. It's a long trip. Are you up for it?"*

"Yes," Ben said. "But why can't you tell me here?"

Rose read his lips and squeezed his shoulders. Her face looked sad and complicated. Ben understood that the only thing he could do was follow her and wait for her to tell him what he wanted to know.

"Are you ready?"

Ben rubbed the smooth silver locket around his neck and nodded.

He was ready.

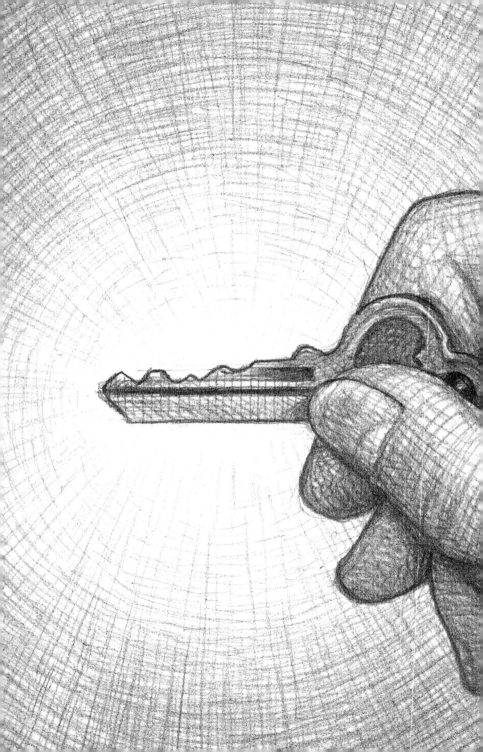

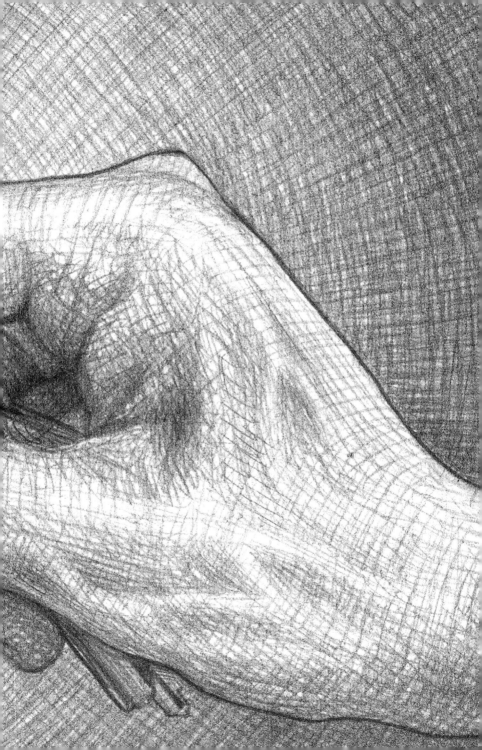

They entered the lobby of the museum, and Rose turned on the lights, motioning for Ben to sit down on a bench. It was hot and stuffy inside. Rose sat beside Ben, then retrieved Ben's notebook and pen from her bag. *"It's going to take me a long time to write this story for you. I need you to be patient with me. Okay? I've never written this all down for anyone."*

A story? Ben didn't want a story. He wanted to meet his dad. Still, he nodded and continued reading as fast as she wrote, line after line, in the notebook.

"I've worked here for fifteen years. But the story I need to tell you begins a long time before that.

"When I was little, I could see New York from my window, but my parents never let me go there. Too dangerous for a deaf girl to leave the house, they said! So, as a child, I used to write little notes and send them out into the world because I felt so alone. I ran away from home many times, and it was Walter who finally rescued me. I found him at the AMNH. . . ."

Ben tapped Rose's shoulder and pointed to *AMNH.* He didn't know what that was.

"American Museum of Natural History."

Of course. Ben nodded for her to go on.

"I knew Walter had gotten his first job selling books at the museum, as part of a new exhibition."

Ben tapped Rose. He mimed opening a book and mouthed the word "Wonderstruck."

Rose nodded. *"I was twelve when I ran away to New York. Walter found me while I was hiding in the exhibition room. Later he took me to his apartment and gave me the book. I've loved museums and cabinets of wonders ever since. I begged him to help me, to get me out of the house, away from our father. I wanted to stay in New York City. I wanted to learn things!*

"At Walter's apartment, I remember gazing out at the gigantic buildings at night. They were so beautiful. I had spent so much time looking at the city from across the water in Hoboken that I was ecstatic to finally be in the middle of it.

"Walter helped find me a school for deaf children. I didn't even know such a thing existed! Our parents were married when my mother was very young. She gave birth to Walter when she was only seventeen. I came along eight years later, and soon after that, my parents divorced. It was a very big scandal back then because my mother was famous (one day I'll show you my scrapbook). Our parents resisted letting me go, but my brother fought with them and convinced them I needed to be at a good boarding school, where everyone was deaf.

"Until I went to school, I had never met another deaf

person. I didn't know it, but this was what I had been waiting for! There were so many people like me! Unfortunately, I didn't like our classes because we were forced to lip-read and speak, which I hated to do and was never good at before I went to school. I had a lipreading and speech tutor at home but I hated him. Once, I cut up his big book and turned it into paper buildings so I wouldn't have to practice!

"But the other students taught me how to sign when we were not in class, and the world opened up. I discovered I could really communicate and make jokes! I never knew how much fun it was to make jokes and laugh with other people! I was never happier.

"At that same school, I met the boy who would become your grandfather, Bill Lobel. He was the handsomest boy in my class, strong, good at sports. Like so many of our classmates, he worked with big machines, on a printing press. Deaf people aren't bothered by the noise, of course, so in those days many of the deaf boys learned how to be printers. I, too, needed a job after I graduated. Walter helped me get work at the AMNH, in the exhibitions department. I'd always loved making things with my hands, and I was so happy to work there, helping to create miniatures of Indian pueblos, Mexican villages, and Arabian cities.

"Bill and I got married after we finished school. Many people, especially our parents, thought it was a bad idea for two deaf people to get married. Everyone worried we would pass our deafness on to our children. But Bill became deaf from an illness when he was nine years old, and no one was sure how, or when exactly, I became deaf. It might have been how I was born, although my father, a doctor, always said it happened when I was two and had a bad fall. Bill's parents, like mine, had a hard time coping with a deaf child. He had five older siblings, all of whom could hear, so no one paid him much attention. But at school he blossomed just as much as I did.

"When I became pregnant, I wondered what it would be like to have a deaf baby. . . . I knew we could give him the upbringing we had missed before we got to our school. But it isn't easy being deaf, and we were happy Danny could hear. That just made everyone even more worried, though! How could two deaf people raise a hearing baby? Our parents pointed out that we couldn't hear a deaf baby OR a hearing baby crying at night. Even worse to them, they worried the baby would never learn to speak. Well, it was hard, but with the help of friends, the voices on the radio, which we left on all the time, and yes, even our parents, we did it, and we loved Danny more than anything."

Rose paused and massaged her writing hand as Ben

caught up. Everything seemed to vanish for him except the pen, the paper, and the story.

"Even though he could hear, I don't think it was easy for Danny. In many ways he ended up in the same position Bill and I were in growing up. We were so different from our parents. But Danny became a child of two worlds, the hearing and the Deaf. He could sign so beautifully, better than many deaf people. Once he was old enough, he sometimes had to act as interpreter for us out in the world, translating between sign language and spoken language. But he never complained. He was a happy child and happiest when he was drawing.

"He loved to paint pictures of animals, and he built the most wonderful little sculptures. He often came to the museum with me when he was growing up. He'd sit next to me in the model-making department, working on his own little projects while I worked on mine. The staff members gave Danny the run of the place and taught him about every aspect of the museum. Soon he had fallen in love with geography and science and math as well as art. They let him play in the half-finished dioramas and the storage rooms."

Ben's hand went into his pocket and he carefully pulled out the seashell turtle. Rose's eyes grew wide when he handed it to her, and he could tell from her expression that she knew exactly what it was. She turned it over in her palm before returning it to Ben.

He took the notebook and pen. *"My mom gave me the turtle when I was going into third grade. She used to call me Turtle because I was shy. She never told me it was from my dad."*

Rose smiled and took back the pen and notebook. *"After the Wonderstruck exhibition closed, they were going to tear it down, but they never got around to it. As the years went by, the room collected dust and slowly it turned into a storage room. Your dad used to hide inside the cabinet, which is where he found the seashell turtle. He loved that turtle and used to carry it around in his pocket."*

Ben smiled, imagining his father giving the turtle, one cold winter's night, to his mom.

Returning it to his own pocket, he gestured for Rose to continue the story.

She drew an arrow going back to the words *the half-finished dioramas and the storage rooms*—and then went on. *"The staff showed Danny what went into creating every aspect of the dioramas. The museum was the one place he wanted to work when he grew up, and once he was old enough, they were eager to hire him. We were so proud.*

"I worked there for many years, several of them along-side Danny. But in 1962, planning was under way for the

1964 World's Fair, which was to be held in Queens. Coun-
tries from all over the world would be participating. There
were going to be shows, rides, and all sorts of attractions.
One of those attractions was going to be a scale model of the
entire city of New York, all five boroughs, all 895,000
buildings. It would be almost 10,000 square feet—the
largest architectural model ever built. They named it the
Panorama, and they needed people to create and glue down
all the buildings and carve the parks and hills.

"When I found out about a job opening, I jumped at
the chance to take it. I was sad to leave the AMNH after so

many wonderful years, but I couldn't say no. As a child, dreaming about New York, I'd built the city out of paper in my room, so in a way I had been preparing for this job my entire life. I worked on the model of New York for two years. I made hundreds of tiny buildings, apartment towers, museums, stores. It was heaven."

Rose stopped to rub her hand again. Then she got up, took Ben's hand, and led him into a dark, cavernous space. She pressed a few buttons in a control panel hidden in the wall, and suddenly a giant spotlight lit up the room.

The Panorama was one of the most wondrous things Ben had ever seen. As they slowly walked around the perimeter, he just stared, taking in all the glorious details. When they reached the top of the ramp that surrounded the model, Rose stopped to write again.

"A few years after it was built, the 1964 World's Fair was closed and dismantled. But they decided to keep the Panorama on display because it was so popular. They needed someone to maintain the model and update it, to

build tiny versions of all the new buildings in New York as they went up, and take away the old ones as they were torn down. They offered me the job."

Around them, the room began to grow dim. Ben looked at Rose, worried. She smiled. *"Every fifteen minutes, night falls,"* she explained.

Ten million tiny windows, painted with little dabs of fluorescent paint, lit up across the darkening city. The model glowed magnificently.

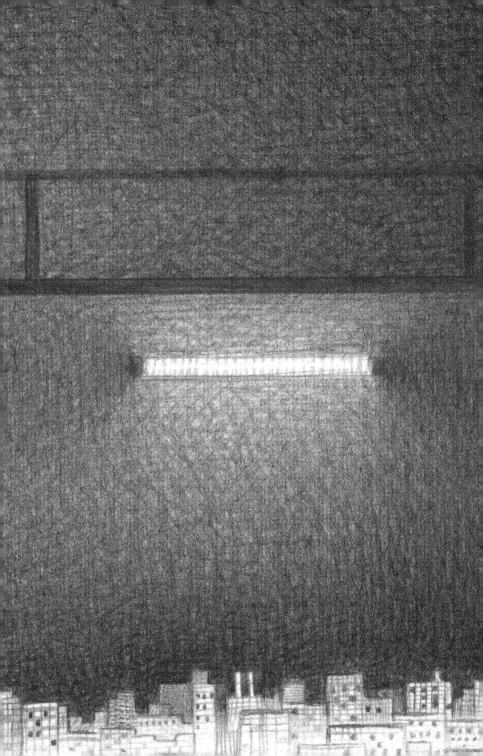

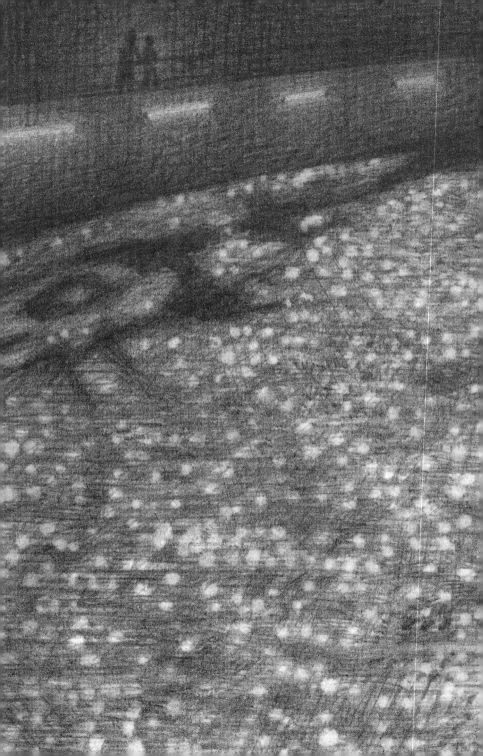

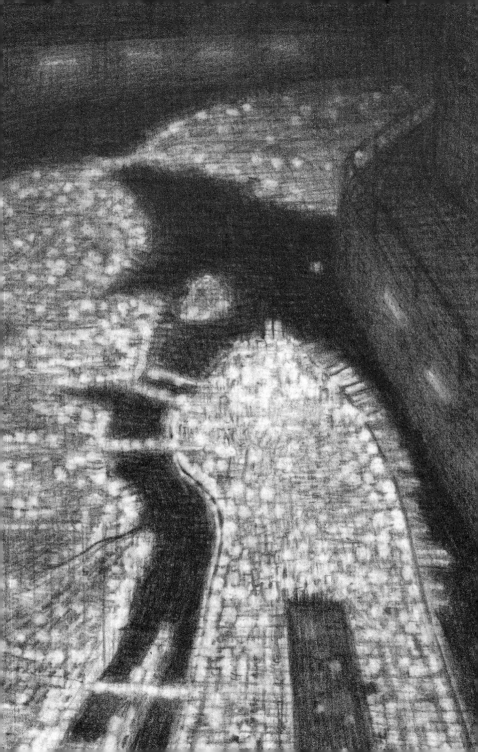

Rose guided Ben down around the pathway surrounding the model as an artificial morning spread across the miniature city.

She wrote the names of all the parts of the city: Manhattan, the Bronx, Staten Island, Brooklyn, and Queens. She pointed out the little version of another holdover from the 1964 World's Fair: the huge silver model of the earth they'd passed on the way here, called the Unisphere. She showed him the small model of the building they were standing in right now, as well as skyscrapers and bridges, green rolling parks and twisting black roads, marshes, graveyards, and power plants. Ben felt like a bird flying above the sprawling expanse of New York City.

When they came to a doorway Ben hadn't noticed before, Rose took out her key ring, opened the door, and led them through. There was a second door at the bottom of a short set of stairs. Rose led Ben through that as well. Then, like giants, the two of them stepped out onto the Atlantic Ocean.

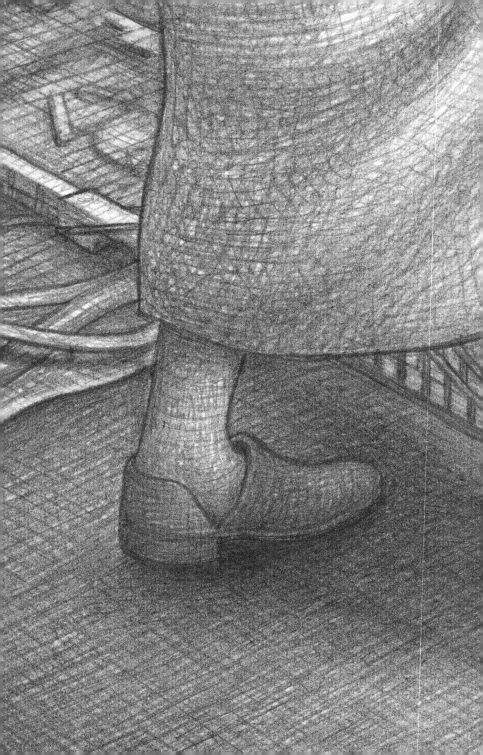

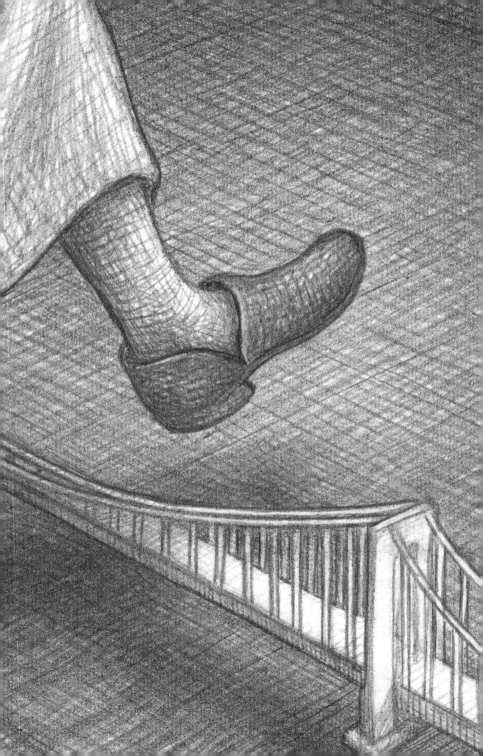

Midway up the East River, after stepping over three more bridges, Rose stopped to write. Standing beside her, between Manhattan and Brooklyn, Ben looked away from the notebook and located Central Park, the Museum of Natural History, the Hayden Planetarium, and the Port Authority.

Night fell again. Ben noticed how parts of their clothing, the whites of Rose's eyes and teeth, and the paper in his notebook glowed purple in the ultraviolet night. They waited without moving until the electric sun rose once more. Ben looked at the notebook, where Rose continued to write.

"I loved helping to create this model. Sometimes, during those two years, I'd stay late into the night after everyone else had left, just so I could be alone with it for a little while. Danny and I would get together and I'd tell him how progress was going and he'd tell me about his latest projects. Around that time, he was appointed the lead designer on a new diorama at the AMNH, the youngest person ever to have that honor.

"But you already know this part, Ben. He headed up to Gunflint Lake, with two other employees of the museum. The two other men found rooms in the big lodge on the lake, but Danny wanted some privacy to work. The librarian he'd contacted to help with their research

happened to co-own a small cabin with her sister, and he rented it from her."

Ben pictured his dad staying in the cabin where he and his cousins had played pirates and monsters, and it made him happy to know he'd walked on the same floor and sat on the same chairs as his dad.

"He spent a lot of time in the area and eventually decided he'd like to focus on the wolves. If you've been through the files, then you've seen many of the drawings. He also sent me some of them, along with wonderful letters. He fell in love with your mom almost immediately. He described her in the most vivid terms. She was unlike anyone he had ever met. He said he always thought librarians were old women in sweaters, but Elaine was very young and beautiful and didn't much care what anyone around her said about her. He used the word 'radical' to describe her, meaning, I think, that she lived completely on her own terms, and he loved that about her. His letters called her independent, unwilling to compromise, a woman of the lake and of books."

It was peculiar, thought Ben, to see his own mother described so perfectly by someone he'd never met.

"But they both knew it couldn't work out. Elaine wouldn't leave Gunflint Lake, and Danny wouldn't move out of New York. He said he always had the sense that

Elaine didn't need a husband or want one. She said she had everything she needed on the lake and in the library. He did think there was something lonely about her, although he wasn't sure what it was she was missing.

"When Danny finished his research on Gunflint Lake, he came back to New York, brokenhearted. I think he'd been happiest when he was there, working on the diorama, falling in love with your mom." Rose stopped writing for a moment, and Ben didn't breathe until her pen started moving again.

"Eventually, he completed the diorama of the wolves, the only one he got to make. I still go visit it whenever I can."

"I saw you there," wrote Ben. *"The other day."*

Rose looked surprised.

"Why didn't my dad get to make more dioramas?" Ben continued. But even as he wrote this, he began to understand what the answer had to be.

Rose paused and looked into Ben's eyes before taking the pen from him. *"Your dad was ill, Ben. He had a heart condition. I don't know if he told your mother. It kept him out of the war, which I was happy about. But a few years after he returned from Gunflint Lake . . . his heart"*—

Rose didn't finish the sentence, and Ben didn't need her to. He covered his face with his hands and was swallowed up in the darkness. He felt Rose reach her arms around him and draw him in. She held him for a long time, and neither of them moved, except for the rise and fall of their chests as they breathed. Ben could tell Rose was crying, too.

After a while, Ben wiped his eyes and said, "Did he know about me?"

Rose read his lips. *"I don't know. I don't think so. But I do know he would have loved you if he had. He adored children. He used to lead tours around the museum for school groups."*

Rose brushed the hair from Ben's forehead and wiped the tears from his cheek.

Ben took the pen. *"But you said you met me before. If my dad didn't know me, how did you?"*

"We're not at the end of the story, Ben. There's something else I want to share with you now. A secret." Rose paused, and Ben moved a little closer to her, waiting anxiously for her to continue.

"This Panorama isn't just a model of the city. It's also the story of your father. That's why I brought you here."

Ben looked out across the endless expanse of miniature buildings. He returned his gaze to the notebook, where Rose continued to write.

"When I took the job here, I thought it would be fun to

secretly personalize the Panorama. So I collected things that had belonged to your father, little mementos from his childhood mostly, and I hid them inside buildings all across the model. Maybe there was a part of me, knowing his heart was weak, that wanted something of him to always be here. That's not how I thought of it at the time, though. I just loved your father and wanted to do this for him and for myself. When I told him about my little project, he helped me curate it, and gave me more things to put into it. In a way, this model tells the story of your father's life in New York. It was like we were making our own cabinet of wonders."

Ben remembered reading about curators in *Wonderstruck*, and thought about what it meant to curate your own life, as his dad had done here. What would it be like to pick and choose the objects and stories that would go into your own cabinet? How would Ben curate *his* own life? And then, thinking about his museum box, and his house, and his books, and the secret room, he realized he'd already begun doing it. Maybe, thought Ben, we are all cabinets of wonders.

"Here is the hospital where your father was born." Rose pointed to a tiny gray brick building. *"Inside I placed a photograph of me and Bill holding him as a baby. Here is the school he went to."* She pointed to a low white building

on the near side of the park. *"I hid one of his pencils there."* Rose continued to point around the model, all across Manhattan, into Brooklyn and Queens, as she told Ben the story of his father's life and explained each of the little artifacts she'd hidden in the places that had been important to him: A lucky penny he found in Central Park was now under the small version of the rectangular green park, a silver charm he'd won at Coney Island rested under the miniature Wonder Wheel that Rose had built, and one of his baby teeth was hidden inside the grocery store where he'd lost it many years ago.

Night descended again across the giant room. Ben noticed a tiny airplane taking off from a tiny airport nearby. It flew to the ceiling on a nearly invisible wire, looped overhead across the city, and then came in for a landing. A few moments later it flew up and repeated the journey.

When day came again, the model was no longer an endless expanse of unknown buildings. It opened up and came to life around Ben, and for a few moments, it was as if his father came to life around him, too.

Ben looked at the model of the Museum of Natural History. He tapped Rose's shoulder. "What is inside *that?*"

She motioned for him to follow her around the

southern tip of Manhattan. They stepped back over the Williamsburg Bridge, the Manhattan Bridge, and the Brooklyn Bridge, and headed up the other side of the island, along the Hudson River, until they were standing on the blue painted water that separated Manhattan from New Jersey.

Rose leaned over the west side of Manhattan, gripped the model of the museum, and pulled upward. There was a little resistance, but it gave way. Rose turned the building over and picked out two pieces of paper. She unfolded the first one and handed Ben a drawing of the wolves that looked just like the ones in the museum files.

"This is one of the drawings Danny sent me." She unfolded the other piece of paper. It was a crude child's drawing but it was recognizable as the wolf diorama. To his astonishment, it was signed *Ben*.

"When your dad died, we had the memorial service at the museum. I knew everyone except for two people: a woman and a little boy who was around four. The woman introduced herself to me using sign language and said her name was Elaine. She told me Danny had been a friend of hers some years ago, and had explained that his parents were both deaf. He'd taught her a little sign language."

Ben marveled at the idea of his mother knowing sign language. She'd never shared it with him, although, now that he thought about it, there had been a few times he'd seen her alone on the couch, not knowing she was being watched, moving her hands through the air. Had she been secretly signing to Danny?

"I knew exactly who she was from the letters. She introduced me to her son, and I was struck by how much the boy looked like Danny when Danny was young. She told me that she'd brought her son to the museum early, and they had visited the diorama Danny made.

"Of course, that boy was you. She squeezed your hand and you reached into your pocket and pulled out a folded piece of paper, which you handed to me. I unfolded it and started to cry. You had drawn the wolves and said I could keep it."

Ben remembered none of this, but in some strange way, it all made sense. His need to collect things, his interest in museums, the wolf dreams . . . it all came into focus sort of like one of those Polaroid pictures from Jamie's camera. Ben's dreams hadn't come from no-where. He'd been dreaming of his *father's* wolves, which he'd *seen.*

He thought about his past few dreams, how silent they were and how he couldn't tell if the wolves were behind him anymore. Finally, he understood that all this time the wolves hadn't been *chasing* him, they'd been *guiding* him, leading him onward, through the snow, to his father.

As Rose folded the two pieces of paper and slipped them back into the tiny museum, Ben reached into his pocket and took out the seashell turtle.

"Can this go in there, too?"

Rose read his lips and smiled.

Ben set the turtle gently on her palm, and carefully, she placed it inside the museum along with the two other treasures.

She returned the museum to the Panorama and continued to write.

"Elaine never said that you were Danny's son, but Bill and I couldn't help but wonder. I remembered Danny's descriptions of her, and it made sense that even if she didn't want a husband, she might still want a child. Maybe that was the one thing she had been missing. You."

Ben blinked and took a deep breath.

If his mom understood how it felt to be missing something, he thought, why wouldn't she talk to him about the one thing *he* had been missing? Was she afraid that he'd want to leave the lake, like Danny? Was it hard for her to watch her son collect things and discover an interest in museums and have so much in common with his dad? She must have thought she was protecting him, or protecting herself from losing him. Either way, Ben felt he understood it now.

"Your mother kept you to herself, but Bill and I couldn't stop thinking about you. So one night we snuck in here and hid your drawing inside the museum."

Ben tapped Rose and mouthed the words, "Where is Bill?"

Rose touched Ben's hand for a moment before writing, *"He died two years ago. I wish you had known each other. He was funny. He liked to play practical jokes. He loved to read. He was proud of the printing press he worked on. And he loved Danny. He would have loved you so much."* Rose shook her head and seemed to laugh a little to herself. *"Oh, Ben! All this time I've wondered if it was true! If we really had a grandson, if you really were Danny's son!"*

Ben reached up and moved his hand slowly across Rose's cheek. It was odd to touch his grandmother's face, almost as if her skin were somehow a part of his own face, and his father's. He thought about how much he missed his mom's touch.

Ben still didn't know if she had planned this trip to New York or if it was just an accident that he'd found the book, and the bookmark, and his grandmother. And that's when it hit him. . . .

"*What is today's date?*" he wrote.

"*July 13. Why?*"

"*Tomorrow is my birthday.*"

Rose's eyes sparkled.

"*Will you teach me sign language?*" Ben wrote.

Rose raised her right hand and moved her fist up and down several times as she nodded.

Ben understood and laughed.

"Thank you for being so brave," Rose wrote. *"Your parents would have been very proud of you."*

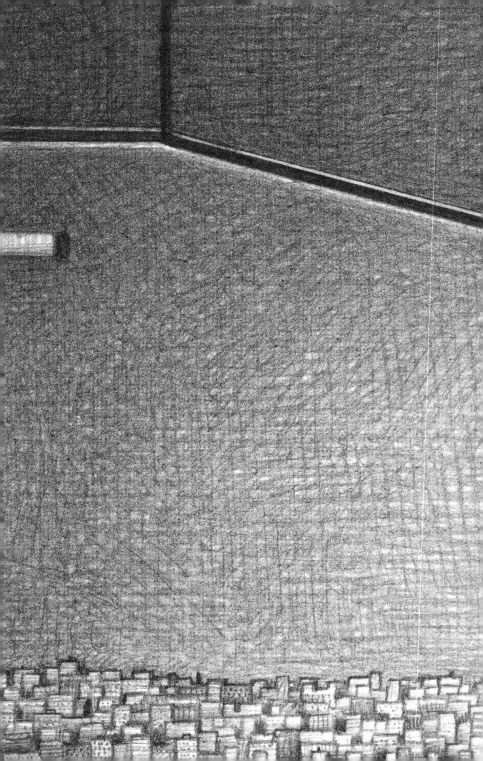

The room was suddenly plunged into complete darkness! The ultraviolet lights didn't come on and everything was submerged in black. Ben felt a terrible panic rise up in him. What had happened? Except for the touch of his grandmother's hand and the floor beneath his feet, everything in the world seemed to disappear.

Ben tried to visualize the tiny city spread out around him. One wrong move and they would crush a bridge or destroy an entire city block. He worried about falling, or worse, Rose falling. How would he get help?

Rose tightened her grip and slowly urged Ben along. Inch by inch, they moved as if they were struggling beneath a black velvet blanket. For a split second, a distant flash of lightning lit the entrance to the Panorama, which opened out to the front doors of the museum. A storm must have begun. Ben shuddered and prayed the building would not be hit.

Rose and Ben shuffled along with tiny footsteps, careful to stay on the river. Ben wiped his face with his T-shirt. Arms extended, they continued to walk through the thick darkness, being careful not to crush any bridges or buildings. After what felt like hours, they bumped into a wall. They groped along it until, with the help of another flash of lightning, Ben located the door. One step at a time they made their way up the dark stairs and onto the walkway surrounding the Panorama. In the distance, lightning flashed again from the entrance.

It grew brighter as they exited the Panorama and headed toward the lobby. Blood pounded in Ben's head. He clutched Rose as a dazzling blast illuminated the lobby and left a glowing aftershock that hurt his eyes.

After a few moments, the lightning stopped. Ben's eyes adjusted to the darkness and at last he understood. There was no storm and there was no lightning. It was *Jamie* on the other side of the glass door, holding his camera and waving madly. Ben knew at once he must have been trying to get their attention with the camera flash since banging on the door obviously hadn't worked. A pile of developing photographs lay at his feet.

Ben rushed to the door and motioned for Rose to open it. Night had fallen, but the streetlamps were dark and the light above the entrance had failed to come on. Rose fished the key from her bag and opened the door. Jamie looked at Rose, and a moment of confusion passed across his face before he threw his arms around Ben.

"How did you get here?" asked Ben.

"I followed you," mouthed Jamie.

Rose pulled the boys away from the door and relocked it. She slowly led them through long hallways, up dark stairs, and to Ben's surprise, out onto the roof. They sat near the edge of the building and caught their breath.

A warm breeze blew gently through their hair as they turned and looked across the river to Manhattan.

To Ben's amazement, the blackout extended across the entire city. The skyline looked like a miniature silhouette. The only difference between the actual city in front of them and the Panorama they'd left behind seemed to be the sky that arched magnificently above them.

Jamie looked from Ben to Rose and back again. Ben could see him trying to talk to Rose, but she was reaching into her bag and didn't notice. She pulled out Ben's notebook and pen and wrote something, which she handed to Jamie with a curious smile. The words were just visible in the moonlight.

"Who are you?"

Ben read the notebook over Jamie's shoulder and said to him, "I think I can answer."

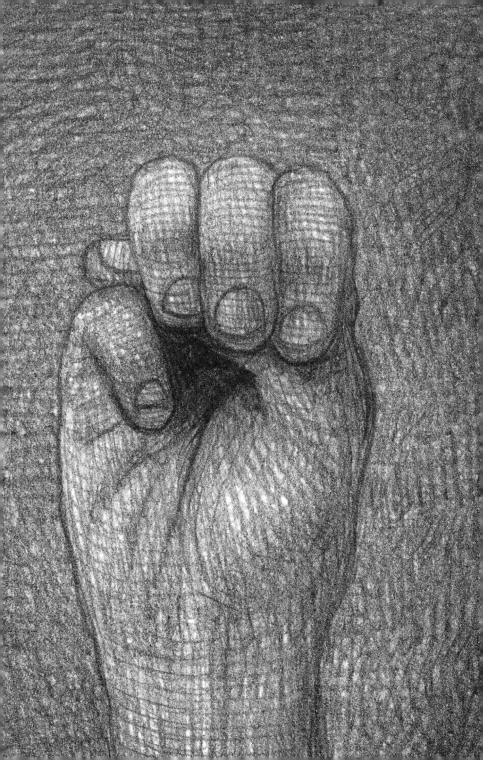

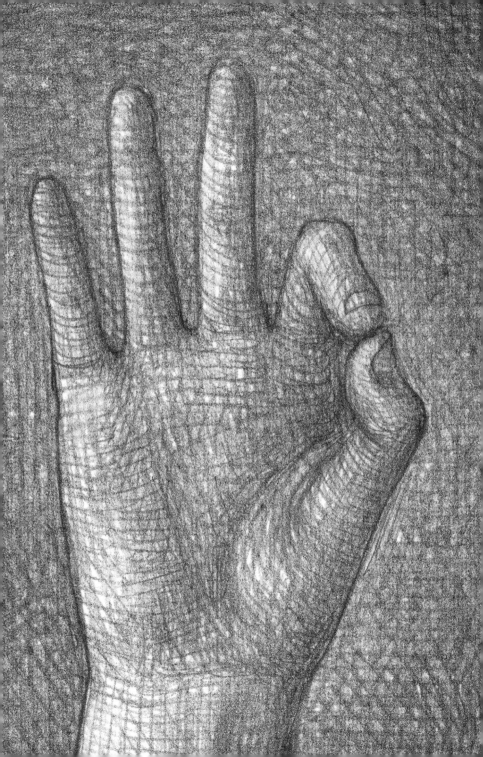

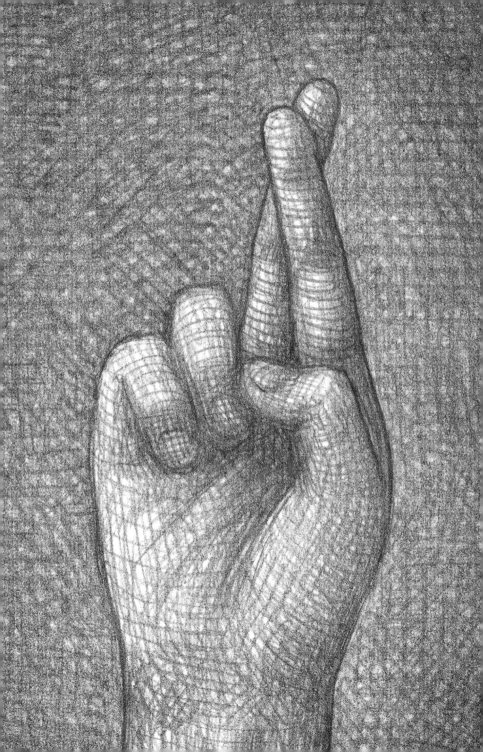

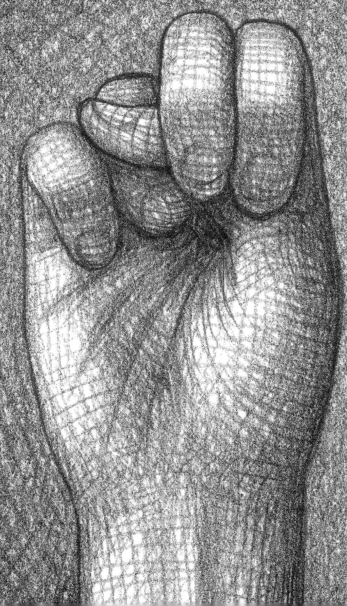

Ben could feel the letters vibrating on his fingers. *My friend.*

Jamie smiled and then finger spelled his name for Rose. She shook his hand.

"This is Rose, my grandmother," Ben told Jamie.

Jamie's jaw dropped. He smiled his crooked grin, and Ben could tell he wasn't sure if Ben was joking. "Really?" he mouthed.

Ben flipped through the notebook and showed Jamie the pages that Rose had written for him.

"Later you will read this. It explains everything." As he said these words, Ben realized how true they were. Not only did the notebook contain the story of his dad and his grandparents but also the story he'd written for Jamie about his mom, and his aunt and uncle and cousins, and Jamie's story about *his* parents, the museum, and bits and pieces of almost all their conversations.

Thinking about all the connections that led him here, Ben marveled at how everything could be traced, like the path on a treasure map, from a book, a turtle, and a cabinet in an old exhibition, to Walter to Rose to Danny to Elaine and then, finally, to Ben himself.

And of course Ben would never have discovered the path in the first place if it weren't for Jamie. The world was full of wonders.

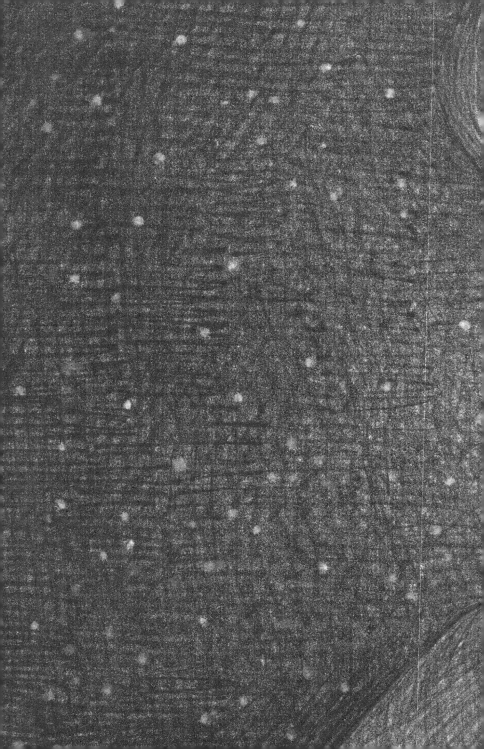

Ben asked Jamie, "Does your dad know where you are?"

Jamie shook his head.

"He's going to worry about you!"

Ben turned to a blank page and wrote, *"How long will the blackout last? Jamie forgot to tell his dad where he was going."*

Rose read it and looked for a moment at Jamie. *"My brother knows where we are,"* she answered. *"He'll come get us in his car and we'll take you home. It will be okay. All we can do right now is wait."*

Ben put his arm on Jamie's shoulder, and Jamie smiled.

Ben looked out at the jagged skyline and wondered what happened in a city without electricity. He'd been scared during the blackout in Minnesota when he was trapped by the storm in his house, but it had given him the chance to read *Wonderstruck* by flashlight in his mom's bed. Ben imagined all of New York City reading by flashlight in their beds, and he marveled over how much had happened from blackout to blackout.

Ben was sure his aunt and uncle had been called by now, but he hoped he wouldn't have to go back to Gunflint Lake right away. Rose had introduced him to the Panorama, as well as to his father's life, and now he was ready to explore the city itself. Maybe he could stay with his grandmother for a while, or maybe, like Jamie, he could come for the summers. Whatever happened, Ben knew that he belonged *here*, with his friend, and his grandmother, and the millions of other people waiting in the dark for the lights to come back on.

Jamie leaned against Ben, and Ben leaned against Rose, and the three of them sat together on the roof of the museum, looking at the stars.

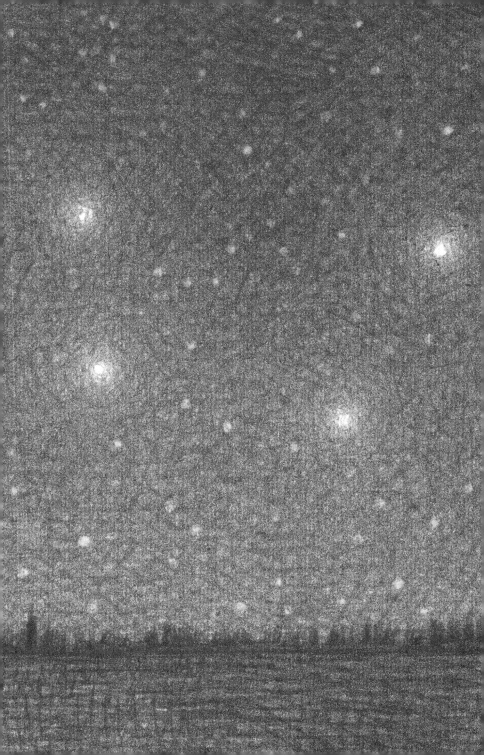

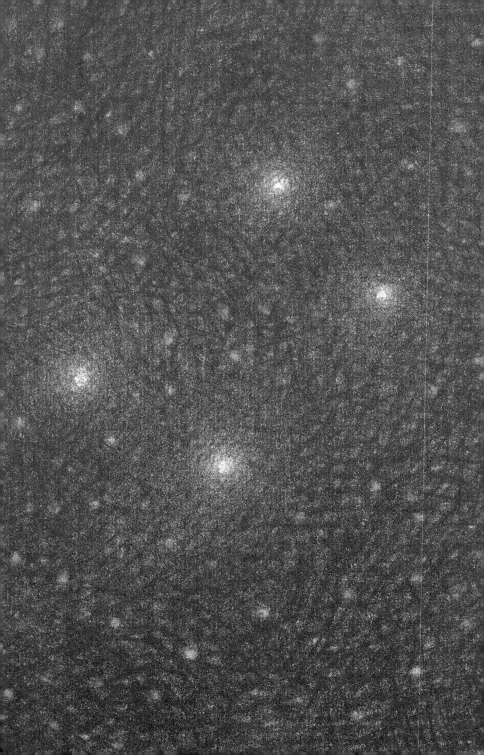

THE

END

ACKNOWLEDGMENTS

While I was working on *The Invention of Hugo Cabret*, I saw a documentary called *Through Deaf Eyes*, about the history of Deaf culture in America (Note: *deaf* with a lowercase *d* refers to the condition of being deaf, while *Deaf* with a capital *D* refers to the culture). I was especially fascinated by a section about cinema and the new technology of sound, which was introduced into the movies in 1927. Prior to this, both deaf and hearing populations could enjoy the cinema together. Sound movies, for the first time, excluded the deaf. That insight was the beginning of Rose's story. The documentary also featured an interview with a young deaf man who was raised by hearing parents, as many deaf people are. It wasn't until he went to college and met other deaf people that he felt he had really found his community. That fascinated me, and I became intrigued by the idea of looking for one's culture outside of one's biological family.

The main seed for *Wonderstruck*, however, was planted many years ago by my friend Sean Murtha, who worked at the American Museum of Natural History in New York City. In the early 1990s, Sean invited me to a backstage tour of the museum, and I was, quite simply, wonderstruck. I thought to myself, "One day I have to set a story here."

I am very grateful to Sean and to so many people who assisted me in my research for *Wonderstruck*, including Sean's colleague at the museum, Carl Mehling, collections manager for the Fossil Amphibian, Reptile, and Bird Collection in the Division of Paleontology, as well as Tom Baione, Mary DeJong, Kathleen Maguire, Barbara Mathé, Mai Qaraman, Stephen Quinn, Eleanor Schwartz, and Ellen Silberman, who also helped with my research at the AMNH.

My drawings of the museum are based closely on archival images from 1927. During my research, I found or re-created the actual floor plans of the museum from 1927 and 1977 so I would know where everything was *supposed* to be. But then, as necessary, I moved or changed things. For instance, in 1927, Ahnighito was located in the room where you entered on Seventy-seventh Street. But because I wanted Rose to wander around the museum for a while before she finds the meteorite, I moved it (much easier for me to do than it was for the museum, which moved it several times). I also located an actual report issued by the museum in 1927 and used some of the language to help write the opening text of Ben's copy of *Wonderstruck*. Also, some of the murals in the museum were inspired by the work of Charles R. Knight.

Deidre Scherer, a fabric artist living in Vermont, grew up visiting her father, Fred, at the AMNH, where he began working in the 1930s. Deidre shared her memories of climbing through the half-finished dioramas her father was still painting. My friend Sevanne Martin grew up visiting the museum in the 1970s to see her grandmother Margaret Meade, the world-famous anthropologist, who had an office there for many years. Vanni also put me in touch with her mother, Dr. Catherine Bateson, who shared her own stories of visiting the museum as a child.

For years, my favorite diorama at the museum has been the wolves in the Hall of North American Mammals. I eventually learned more about James Perry Wilson, the artist who painted the diorama backdrop, and gave Ben his last name. I traveled to Minnesota to see the setting of Wilson's diorama myself. I was delighted to find that the nearest town to Gunflint Lake, Grand Marais (an hour away), is a haven for artists. The town librarian, Anne Prinsen, told me a lot about life in the area. She took my partner and me around town and showed us the library and many other places my characters would have known. Through Anne, I met a local artist and children's book illustrator, Betsy Bowen, who helped me immensely by sharing her memories of Grand Marais, as did Stephen Hogeland, a local jewelry designer from whom we rented a room. No one in town seemed to know that behind a large glass window in a museum in New York City, there exists a little slice of their corner of Minnesota, frozen forever in artificial blue moonlight.

Gunflint Lodge, where Ben's aunt and uncle work, has been owned since 1929 by the family of Bruce Kerfoot and his wife, Sue. I learned from them that the entire Gunflint Lake region was formed billions of years ago by the impact of a meteorite. While this discovery wasn't actually made until very recently, I decided to have Ben learn about it in the 1970s since it worked so well with my story. Mark Jirsa of the Minnesota Geological Survey filled me in on the details of the real meteorite and the stones of the area.

Back on the East Coast, David Levithan gave me a tour of his town, Hoboken, New Jersey. We stopped at the Hoboken Historical Society as well as the Stevens Institute of Technology. The model for Rose's house can be found on the campus there, on a cliff looking out over Manhattan, just as it does in the book.

Cary Stumm at the New York Transit Museum helped me ensure the subways and elevated trains in the story are as accurate as possible.

I first visited the Queens Museum of Art about four years ago and fell in love with the Panorama. Louise Weinberg and Arnold Kanarvogel took me on a rare trip out onto the surface of the Panorama itself. Tom Finkelpearl, the executive director of the museum, has also been very supportive of the project from the very beginning.

The blackout really did begin on July 13, 1977, as it does in my story. Ben wouldn't have known the cause of the blackout, but later he would find out that the power grid had been hit by lightning.

Dr. Mary Ann Cooper, one of the country's leading specialists on lightning strike injuries, read the manuscript and helped me understand the impact of a strike, and how patients would deal with their injuries. My brother, Dr. Lee Selznick, was born deaf in one ear like Ben. It was fascinating to talk to him about this now. Many of Ben's observations and thoughts on the subject come from my brother.

Since I knew early on that both of my main characters would be deaf, I wanted to learn as much as possible about Deaf culture. I read books, conducted interviews, and had conversations with people who are deaf or who are experts on aspects of Deaf culture. My partner's colleagues at the University of California, San Diego, Carol Padden (who became a MacArthur Fellow in 2010) and her husband, Tom Humphries, are two of the leading experts in the country on Deaf culture and linguistics, and they were generous enough to read the manuscript at various stages and share personal stories about their own childhoods. They gave me valuable insights into the history of Deaf culture, pointed me toward texts to help create the book's introduction, "Teaching the Deaf to Lip-Read and Speak," that Rose reads (and which I made up), and helped me better understand how Ben and Rose would interact with the world around them. Rick Rubin, who has worked as an interpreter for Carol and Tom for many years, was a huge help throughout this process, especially when Tom took me to visit the archives of PS 47, a public school for the deaf in Manhattan. Lloyd Shikin, the archivist there and a former student, took us into the classroom he'd converted into a sort of mini-museum, and shared photographs, newspaper articles, and many artifacts about Deaf education in the 1920s and beyond.

Amara Engel talked to me about being a deaf kid who signs, lip-reads, and speaks. She told me about dreaming in sign, and I found the conversation inspiring. Rebecca Freund, a young artist, read the book in manuscript and shared helpful and important insights about growing up deaf. Susan Burch, an associate professor of American studies at Middlebury College, spoke with me about the history of Deaf culture, and Emily Thompson, professor of history at Princeton University, provided valuable information on the transition from silent to sound cinema. Michael Olson, archives preservation specialist at Gallaudet University, also assisted. And I'd be remiss if I didn't mention Remy Charlip, whose book *Handtalk* taught me the sign language alphabet when I was ten.

Of course, any story about kids who run away to a museum owes a debt of gratitude to E. L. Konigsburg's *From the Mixed-up Files of Mrs. Basil E. Frankweiler*. In order to pay back that debt, *Wonderstruck* is filled with references to Konigsburg and her book. How many can you spot? Two other books that were important inspirations were *My Daniel* and *Call Me Ahnighito* by Pam Conrad. Because I imagined Rose as a reader, I gave her two books not published by 1927: *Little House in the Big Woods* by Laura Ingalls Wilder, with its loving family, and *The Moffats* by Eleanor Estes, about a single mother raising four children. Both seemed like the perfect fantasies for Rose. The Moffats series, like *Wonderstruck*, ends in a museum.

The quote "We are all in the gutter, but some of us are looking at the stars" is from the play *Lady Windermere's Fan* by Oscar Wilde.

Many friends and colleagues read my story or helped in one way or another. I have to thank Leslie Budnick, Michael Citrin, Deborah deFuria, Dan Hurlin (whose show *Hiroshima Maiden* inspired the structure for

Wonderstruck), Wendy Lukehart, Michael Mayer, Peter Mendelsund, Ida Pearl, Pam Muñoz Ryan, Dr. Edward Spector, Sarah Weeks, Jacqueline Woodson, Paul O. Zelinsky, and Jonah Zuckerman. Thank you to my niece, Allison Selznick, who drew the flowers and leaves in Ben's copy of *Wonderstruck*, and to my nephews, Brennan, Dillan, and Jordan Spector, who talked to me about the Oscar Wilde quote. The staff at Warwick's Bookstore in La Jolla was endlessly supportive while I worked on this book, especially Jan Iverson and Janet Lutz.

Tony Nichols, Angela Hanka, and Catherine Wagner at Lapis Press went above and beyond the call of duty, and I thank them very much for their scanning and printing expertise. Noel Silverman continues to guide me brilliantly as both lawyer and friend. My gratitude only grows.

Thank you to the MacDowell Colony in Peterborough, New Hampshire, where I spent seven rainy weeks during the summer of 2009, working on this book in a beautiful little cabin in the woods.

The team at Scholastic continues to astound me at every turn with their support and enthusiasm. I have to thank Ellie Berger, Lori Benton, Emellia Zamani, Chelsea Donaldson, Monique Vescia, Joy Simpkins, Karyn Browne, Adam Cruz, Meryl Wolfe, Shannon Rice, Charisse Meloto, Rachel Coun, Stacy Lellos, Leslie Garych, Geoff DeCicco, Risa Wallberg, Steve Alexandrov, Adrienne Vrettos, Norah Forman, Vicki Tisch, Catherine Sisco, John Mason, Lizette Serrano, Tracy van Straaten, Jazan Higgins, and Rachel Horowitz. Thank you to David Saylor and Charles Kreloff for their brilliant design work once again, and to my editor, Tracy Mack, who, to put it simply, is the reason this book exists.

And finally, thanks of course to David Serlin, for everything.

SELECTED BIBLIOGRAPHY

DEAFNESS AND DEAF CULTURE

Baynton, Douglas C. *Forbidden Signs*. University of Chicago Press, 1998

Bragg, Lois, editor. *Deaf World*. NYU Press, 2001

Burch, Susan. *Signs of Resistance*. NYU Press, 2004

Cohen, Leah Hager. *Train Go Sorry*. Vintage, 1995

Davis, Lennard J. *Enforcing Normalcy*. Verso, 1995

Gannon, Jack R. *Deaf Heritage*. National Association for the Deaf, 1981

Groce, Nora Ellen. *Everyone Here Spoke Sign Language*. Harvard University Press, 1985

Lane, Harlan. *When the Mind Hears*. Vintage, 1989

Padden, Carol, and Tom Humphries. *Deaf in America*. Harvard University Press, 1988

Padden, Carol, and Tom Humphries. *Inside Deaf Culture*. Harvard University Press, 2006

Spradley, Thomas S., and James P. Spradley. *Deaf Like Me*. Gallaudet University Press, 1985

Uhlberg, Myron. *Hands of My Father*. Bantam, 2009

Van Cleve, John Vickrey, editor. *The Deaf History Reader*. Gallaudet University Press, 2007

MUSEUMS AND CABINETS OF WONDERS

American Museum of Natural History: The Official Guide 2010, published by the museum

Preston, Douglas J. *Dinosaurs in the Attic*. St. Martin's Press, 1993

Quinn, Stephen C. *Windows on Nature: The Great Habitat Dioramas of the American Museum of Natural History*. Abrams, 2006

Stafford, Barbara Maria, and Frances Terpak. *Devices of Wonder*. Getty Research Institute, 2001

Weschler, Lawrence. *Mr. Wilson's Cabinet of Wonder*. Vintage, 1996

Yates, Frances A. *The Art of Memory*. University of Chicago Press, 1966

CLOTHING AND OBJECTS IN 1927

Blum, Stella, editor. *Everyday Fashions of the Twenties.* Dover, 1981

Mirken, Alan, editor. *1927 Edition of the Sears, Roebuck Catalogue.* Bounty Books, 1970

STAGE AND SCREEN

Appelbaum, Stanley, editor. *The New York Stage: Famous Productions in Photographs.* Dover, 1976

St. Romain, Theresa. *Margarita Fischer.* McFarland & Co. Inc., 2008

WORLD'S FAIRS

Official Guide: New York World's Fair 1964/1965. Time-Life Books

Cotter, Bill, and Bill Young. *Images of America: The 1964–1965 New York World's Fair: Creation and Legacy.* Arcadia Publishing, 2008

SCRAPBOOKS

Helfand, Jessica. *Scrapbooks: An American History.* Yale University Press, 2008

LIGHTNING

Friedman, John S. *Out of the Blue.* Delacorte Press, 2008

GUNFLINT LAKE

Cordes, James Patrick. *The Treasures of Minnesota's North Shore and Gunflint Trail.* Published by the author

Henricksson, John. *Gunflint: The Trail, the People, the Stories.* Adventure Publications, 2003

Kerfoot, Justine. *Gunflint: Reflections on the Trail.* University of Minnesota Press, 2007 (First edition, Pfeifer-Hamilton Publishers, 1991)

Kerfoot, Justine. *Woman of the Boundary Waters.* University of Minnesota Press, 1994 (First edition, Women's Times Publishing, 1986)

HOBOKEN

Colrick, Patricia Florio. *Images of America: Hoboken.* Arcadia Publishing, 1999

INSPIRATIONS

Charlip, Remy, Mary Beth Miller, and George Ancona. *Handtalk*. Simon
& Schuster, 1974

Conrad, Pam. *Call Me Ahnighito*. HarperCollins, 1995

Conrad, Pam. *My Daniel*. HarperCollins, 1991

Konigsburg, E. L. *From the Mixed-up Files of Mrs. Basil E. Frankweiler*.
Atheneum, 1967

DOCUMENTARY FILM

Hott, Lawrence, and Diane Garey. *Through Deaf Eyes*. WETA Washington,
D.C., 2007

WEBSITES

American Museum of Natural History http://www.amnh.org/

Betsy Bowen http://woodcut.com/

Deidre Scherer http://www.dscherer.com/

Gunflint Lodge http://www.gunflint.com/

James Perry Wilson http://www.peabody.yale.edu/james-perry-wilson/

Learn Sign Language http://www.aslpro.com/

Minnesota Geological Survey http://www.mngs.umn.edu/index.html

Museum of Jurassic Technology http://www.mjt.org/

National Association of the Deaf http://www.nad.org/

Queens Museum of Art http://www.queensmuseum.org/

This book is dedicated to Maurice Sendak.

Copyright © 2011 by Brian Selznick
All rights reserved. Published by Scholastic Press, an imprint of Scholastic Inc.,
Publishers since 1920. SCHOLASTIC, SCHOLASTIC PRESS, and associated logos are
trademarks and/or registered trademarks of Scholastic Inc.

Library of Congress Cataloging-in-Publication Data available
ISBN 978-0-545-02789-2
10 9 8 7 6 5 4 3 2 1   11 12 13 14 15
Printed in China   38
First edition, October 2011

*The book was printed on 120 GSM UPM Wood Free paper and was thread-sewn
in 16-page signatures by King Yip (Dongguan) Printing & Packaging Co., Ltd.,China*

*The text of this book was set in 12-point Monotype Bulmer.
The display type was set in P22 Parrish Roman.
Brian Selznick's drawings were created in pencil
on Fabriano Artistico watercolor paper.
The book was designed by Brian Selznick,
David Saylor, and Charles Kreloff.*